Illusions

Barbara Winkes

For D.

Chapter One

The group using the track field for their training, a team of high school girls, had gone over their allotted time.

He had come to this place to look for prey before, with success. The teenage girls didn't interest him, though he knew he'd have to pay attention. The parents and friends might remember him, think there was something strange about the presence of someone who wasn't a father or otherwise relative to one of them.

It could be to his advantage as well, creating an alibi regarding the real reason he spent many of his mornings in places like this. He might have to change territory. Keep them off balance. It wasn't necessary yet, because his mentor had taught him well. No one had even connected the cases yet. Perhaps they never would, because he was too smart for all of them.

He watched as the girl who had passed the finish line first, caught her breath and then headed towards two women sitting in the bleachers, exchanging high fives. He scoffed at the image. They had to be everywhere now, didn't they? He remembered a time when they wouldn't have been so obvious, let alone openly raise a child together. He couldn't hear the words they exchanged, but curiosity made his gaze linger on the scene. One of the women turned around as if she could sense his scrutiny.

He quickly put on his baseball cap and faked a cough, turning away, but he had seen enough.

One of them was the cop that had kept pestering him with questions. He had done well so far, but he could tell she was still fishing. He'd seen the other one at the station as well. What were they doing here? Were they on to him? The girl, was she a plant too? He sat frozen for several moments until the girls' training was over. Most of the spectators were leaving. A few parents who had come early, like him, remained.

As the minutes ticked by, he was starting to relax, realizing that the women's presence had been a coincidence. They had left as well. No one was coming to arrest him.

He leaned back in his seat, trying to focus his mind on the matter at hand. It had been too long since he'd had the opportunity to hunt. With his last case going sideways, the risk had been too high, and he didn't want to go out of town again. Logistics were too complicated, not to mention high costs and gaining the attention of another department. When the next team came in, and no officers had approached him with handcuffs, a smile appeared on his face. Several parents cheered the young men taking over the field. He envied and admired their proud, cocky attitude, wishing he could have been one of them.

These days, he got to teach them.

That was even better.

He zoned in on the one he'd chosen a couple of weeks before, frowning when he saw him standing to the side, the girl who had made the impressive run earlier, talking to him.

He'd have to do more research to be on the safe side, but he wasn't going to change plans.

Those who stood in his way would regret it.

Detective Jordan Carpenter walked onto the crime scene with an air of victory. It was wrong, maybe, to feel that way, but she couldn't help it.

She hadn't missed any important steps in her daughter's young life. Meri had not yet taken any actual steps, but she was starting to pull herself up anywhere she could hold on to, displaying her precarious balance with pride. Finally, Jordan was back on the job.

She wasn't taking either of those things for granted after surviving the attack of a young, confused woman. Joy Anne Deane was consumed by her bigoted anger, and she'd had a knife. With her conviction, they were fortunately done rehashing what happened, and what could have been.

This unusually chilly morning, she stood over the body of a man in his late seventies.

"Cause of death, fairly obvious, I'd say," she mumbled, pushing her cold hands into the pockets of her jeans.

"We'll have to see what the tox screen says, but yes." The medical examiner, Dr. Melissa Adams, glanced at the thick branch only inches away from the man's body. It was encrusted in blood.

"Whether he drank or not, for sure he didn't hit himself over the head with that branch. Repeatedly. If we're lucky, the attacker left a bit of his own DNA." She leaned closer to take a look at the rough bark. Whoever had committed this crime had likely done so in a rage, not taking much care to clean up. They night have nicked their own skin while gripping the branch and...There was a good chance. "Let me know when you're ready?"

"Of course," Dr. Adams confirmed.

After studying the surroundings some more, Jordan went over to Officer Sam Potts who stood to the side with the woman who'd had the misfortune of finding the bloodied body. She had her head turned away from the ghastly scene and looked pale.

"Mrs. Miller, Detective Carpenter," Potts introduced them. "Mrs. Miller is the deceased's neighbor. She was walking her dog."

"I come by here with Buddy every day, but I rarely saw him. Neighbors, it didn't mean all that much. After we introduced ourselves, he barely ever spoke to us," the woman said, her voice trembling. She was holding a small dog in her arms. "My kids were a bit freaked out by him."

"His name is Charles Salter," Sam Potts supplied.

"That house is his?" Jordan looked behind herself to the only house visible in the distance, a farmhouse behind a row of trees.

"Yes. I believe he lived there with his wife and son," Mrs. Miller confirmed. "The wife died a long time ago, and the son moved out shortly thereafter. I met him once. He rarely ever came out here. Very polite unlike his father." She shuddered. "I can't believe I said that. I didn't wish him anything bad. Certainly not that. It's horrible."

"I understand," Jordan said softly. "Aside from his son, do you know if he had seen anyone else lately?"

Mrs. Miller shook her head. "Not that I'm aware of, but that doesn't mean anything. Our house is closer to the road, but still kind of up here in the woods. I thought my husband was foolish to want to relive a childhood fantasy. I hope this will convince him that we have to move out of here."

Jordan couldn't blame her, though she was fairly sure that whoever had targeted the man wasn't interested in the Millers.

"You said your kids were freaked out," she said. "Is there any particular reason? Did he say anything inappropriate to them?"

The woman's eyes widened.

"You don't think...Oh my God."

"Please, just tell me what you meant."

"No, not anything like that. He wasn't very friendly, that's all."

"All right, thank you, Mrs. Miller. I'd like you to come to the station later today to record your statement. Three o'clock?"

Jordan realized it might become necessary to talk to the Millers' children too. She wondered if Salter had indeed been inappropriate with someone's kids, to make them angry enough to go at him with that branch.

"I can do that."

"Good. If you can think of anything else…"

"I'll let you know," Mrs. Miller said, obviously relieved that she'd be able to leave the scene.

"Officer Potts here will drive you home. Sam, afterwards, I'd like you to come back here right away."

Sam nodded and went to accompany Mrs. Miller and the equally distraught puppy to the squad car. Jordan went to join the other officer on the scene, Libby Marshall. "We'll have to bring in a few more people," she said. "I'm thinking there might be a clue inside that house as to what brought this on."

⁜

It wasn't a surprise that they'd been unable to reach Salter's son for far. Jordan had, however, succeeded in getting a search warrant for the property. With Charles Salter listed as the only owner, and the importance of finding clues regarding his murder, A.D.A. Valerie Esposito had cut through any red tape swiftly. They were about to enter the structure that, at a second glance, looked a lot bigger and more rundown than it had from a distance.

Derek Henderson had arrived on the scene as well, which was a surprise.

"I thought you'd be stuck in court all day," Jordan greeted him.

"Good morning to you too. Defense lawyer asked for a continuance, so here I am."

Secretly, Jordan was thrilled about the development. It mattered to her that her closest friends and colleagues could convince themselves that she was back one hundred percent. In the wake of recent events, she had a lot to prove, if mostly to herself.

"You're lucky," she told him. "The fun's about to start."

"That's your idea of fun?" He made a non-committal sound. "If the inside's kept up as badly as the outside, it's going to be more of a health hazard."

She laughed. "You're just worried you're going to get dust on that suit."

"It's a legit concern," Derek said with a shrug. "What else should I know?"

"The neighbor who found him is coming in this afternoon for her statement. We should be done by then. She described him as a somewhat creepy old guy—let's see if that was imagination, or if we find something to back it up."

"Ready when you are."

Jordan had been ready to kick in the rackety door with the spider web cracks in the glass, but instead, she could open it and walk over the creaking threshold. She sneezed.

"Like I said—not much upkeep in here either," Derek commented when they stepped into a living room crammed with old-fashioned furniture. The kitchen was small and closed off, a small bathroom to the side. Officers Potts and Marshall were coming in behind them. "What exactly are we looking for?"

"Anything out of the ordinary."

Potts and Marshall exchanged a look. Jordan had to admit it would be an understatement to call her instructions vague.

"I'll know it when I see it." That wasn't much better, but she couldn't specify much at this moment. "Look, whoever did this, I think they came for him, and there should be hints in here as to why."

"That's a hunch, or...?"

"A hunch so far. Bear with me."

"Don't I always," he grumbled good-naturedly as he opened a cabinet with a gloved hand. Jordan left him to look into one of the bedrooms. It was obvious that the house had never been updated, so it didn't come with a master suite. The main bathroom was further down the hall. As she inspected closets, she could hear the footsteps of the Potts and Marshall, doors opening and closing. She kneeled down to take a look under the bed, wincing at the layer of dust. The bed was made immaculately though, a stark contrast to the dust everywhere. When did Charles Salter step outside? A quick inspection of the mattress didn't reveal any clues, but the desk came with some locked doors and drawers. Jordan looked around for the key, jumping when she heard the scream.

A moment later she joined Derek in the hallway. Libby Marshall came running towards them.

"We were looking at an addition made to the house." Her tone was clipped and urgent. "Sam fell through the floor!"

"What? Is she hurt?"

"Her arm might be broken. She tried to brace herself."

"Okay, show me where. Let's get an ambulance over here."

"Jordan, wait."

Jordan ignored Derek and went into the direction from which Libby had come. Far down the hallway, someone had built an addition to the house which apparently included a basement. A few steps led down from the ground floor to the landing that had given way under Sam's weight.

"Hey, Sam! How are you doing down there?"

"As long as I don't move my arm, it's bearable," Sam called back. Her voice was surprisingly close. Whoever had built this addition—Charles Salter?—had likely neglected to inform themselves about the city's regulations.

"Okay, good. Don't move. The ambulance is on the way."

Jordan tried to get a closer look. "What is down there?" she asked, partly to distract Sam from any pain, partly because she couldn't help thinking this space might somehow be significant.

"Not much," Sam answered. "It's pretty dirty like the rest of it. I doubt this was used for anything. No electricity as far as I can see. Wait."

"What is it?" Jordan asked, strangely excited.

"Get back, or you're going to fall in too," Derek predicted.

"How about you make yourself useful and get me a ladder? They'll have to open it up more anyway to get her out."

"You're kidding, right?"

"I can assure you, I am not."

"Guys? There's some very primitive plumbing." Sam sounded apprehensive all of a sudden. "And, if I'm not mistaken...Bones."

A cold shiver ran down Jordan's spine. This discovery might be completely unrelated to Salter, or his murderer, but she didn't believe it was.

"I'm coming down as soon as Derek finds that latter," she said. Ideally, before the ambulance arrived, and the scene would be even more contaminated. "Hang on, Sam. You'll be out of here in no time."

"I hope so," the young officer returned. "This is starting to creep me out."

Jordan hadn't missed the fact that she'd used the same term Mrs. Miller had earlier.

Derek had relented and produced a ladder they were slowly lowering through the opening Sam's fall had produced.

"I should go."

"No way. I weigh less, and if the rest of this place is any indication, I'm the one who should try that ladder. Just hold on to it." On the other side, Libby Marshall gripped the side of the ladder, and Jordan climbed onto it, satisfied that the rungs held her weight. A moment later, she stepped onto dirt. Concrete had been laid down in only a part of the space—either someone had abandoned the work, or they had use for a softer ground. Like someplace to bury a body. She turned to Sam, who looked miserable, crouched down and squeezed her shoulder.

"Don't worry, they'll be here soon."

"I hope so," Sam said with a shudder. Jordan followed her gaze, and she could see what had raised Sam's concern, something sticking out in the dark ground...

"Stay here," she said unnecessarily.

Sam scoffed. "Where would I go?"

"Sure. Sorry."

Jordan cast another look at what resembled a partially revealed ribcage. What were the odds Charles Salter didn't know about the body buried in the, from the looks of it, hastily and carelessly built addition?

Chapter Two

J ordan and Derek stayed at the house longer than antici-pated, overseeing the disinterring of more bones, and the seizure of evidence from the living quarters.

After Sam had been admitted, she'd checked with the hos-pital to make sure she hadn't suffered any more severe injuries than the clean break and conferred with Dr. Adams on the findings of more human remains on Salter's property.

They returned to the station with minutes to spare for her scheduled interview with the neighbor Mrs. Miller.

Jordan realized she'd never had time for a lunch break. For a moment she thought she was hallucinating the sight of Ellie walking towards her desk with Meri in the stroller.

"Hey," she said after a quick kiss for a greeting. "I heard about Sam, and after I saw her, I realized you might have some use for this."

"You're a lifesaver," Jordan commented with regard to the coffees and muffins Ellie had brought. "We'll be here a little while longer." She leaned forward to kiss Meri's cheek, the girl's resulting laughter filling her with joy even under the circum-stances. Meri reached out her hands, and Ellie picked her up.

"Sorry, but Mommy is busy. We just came by to bring you this and say hi."

"Did you enroll her in the academy yet? Does she have any choice?" Detective Maria Doss, who had joined them, commented. "Hi Meri. How do you feel about helping with Auntie Maria's paperwork?"

Meri made a face as if in reaction.

"All right, I got the message. Is Sam going to be okay?"

"Yes, clean break," Jordan said. "She was just unlucky to be the first to step on that rotten part of the wood, and it gave." She noticed Ellie flinch at her wording. "Anyway, the witness will be here in a few, Melissa's at work downstairs. Any word on the son yet?"

Maria shook her head. "He has an address in town. I left a message."

"I guess this means you won't be home at dinnertime." Ellie didn't phrase it as a question. "Kate's coming over."

"We'll talk later, okay? Thank you for the snacks."

"No problem." Ellie smiled and put Meri back into the stroller. After securing her adequately, she left.

"It's pretty awesome how you manage all of it," Maria commented. "Especially after..."

"My parents helped a lot," Jordan cut her off quickly to avoid the subject her colleagues seemed to slip back into with such ease.

"Yeah, I imagine."

To Jordan's relief, Officer Marshall came by to inform her that Mrs. Miller had arrived. Maria took one of the coffees. "Since Derek isn't here, would you mind if I sit in?"

"I don't expect any groundbreaking news." She winced, thinking it made a rather bad pun under the circumstances. "But of course, feel free."

To Jordan's surprise, Mrs. Miller had brought her family, the husband and two children, a girl of about six years old, and an older, pre-teen boy. Taking in their anxious expressions, Jordan had an idea.

"Thank you so much for coming in," she said. "If you could excuse us for a second." Taking Maria aside, she whispered to her, "I'd like you to talk to the husband and the kids, get their impressions of Salter."

"Sure thing."

To the family, she said, "I know this has been an upsetting day for you, so we'll try to get this over with as quickly as possible. I'm going to take your statement, Mrs. Miller, and Mr. Miller, if you and your children could please go with my colleague? I believe she's got coffee and even hot chocolate."

"I do," Maria said with an encouraging smile. "Please follow me."

"What is this about?" Mrs. Miller said when they were out of earshot. She looked nervous. "I found him. They don't know anything."

"Like I said, I'm sure it's been stressful. I want to make sure we are as accommodating as possible while they have to wait for you."

Reassured, Mrs. Miller smiled. "You've been very kind. Thank you."

"It's a shock. I understand," Jordan said, not committing to the woman's assessment.

❧

If pressed, Ellie would have had to admit that bringing snacks and coffee hadn't been all that was on her mind. For most of the time, she and Jordan would see each other during the day, even if they didn't always work on the same cases. Jordan's parents had a lot to do with that, often taking care of Meri while still running their own business.

Kate and Derek, Meri's Godparents, helped out whenever they could, but they, too, had their own careers to tend to.

Ellie had taken some time to be at home, time that was coming to an end now.

They might have to look into finding daycare for Meri after all, that, and after a little over a week, she felt the need to unobtrusively check up on Jordan.

Things were back to normal, better than fine.

Weren't they?

After the disappointment of a case coming to a premature anti-climactic end, not to mention the traumatic incident that preceded it, Jordan had thrown herself into work. It seemed to help her, and recently, it had given Ellie more time to spend with their daughter. They were lucky that the department was able to accommodate new parents.

She had found nothing out of the ordinary, Jordan and their colleagues being busy with a new case and grateful for the supply of junk food.

"We'll have to teach you better habits, right?" she asked Meri who pursed her lips and shook her head with regard to the spoonful of healthy baby food. Soon enough, they'd start with solids. Raising a child might be the biggest challenge she and Jordan had ever faced together. So far so good. Why was she still worried? Would it ever end?

Kate arrived half an hour later, carrying a bottle of wine.

"I just passed a few important tests, but we should celebrate every day, right? Carpe diem and all. Hey, Meri," she said after hugging Ellie. "Are you ready for a girls' night?"

"She's ready for a nap," Ellie said. "I'm afraid it's just the two of us."

"Yeah, I talked to Derek earlier. New case...They seem busy."

It was strange to realize she knew almost nothing about it. That would likely change once she went back to work full-time, but for the moment, Ellie felt oddly out of the loop. She didn't think Derek had shared many details with Kate at this point.

"Yes, they are."

"What about you? You've been enjoying your time with Meri?" Kate had gone to the kitchen to get a bottle opener.

"Oh yes. We've been lucky the department has been accommodating."

Kate, a frequent guest who knew her way around the house, got two glasses out of the cabinet and came back to join Ellie.

"You've been doing great. She's such a sweetheart. I'll get this ready while you put her to bed."

"Thanks."

By the time Ellie tiptoed out of the room and back downstairs. Kate had a plate with cheese, crackers and grapes ready, and she'd poured each of them a glass of wine.

"And I've been joking about teaching her good habits."

"Well, she's asleep now, and you're still running after the bad guys. I bought a membership for a year at Derek's gym. We have yet to find out if that was a good idea, but you and I have nothing to worry about."

Ellie leaned back into the couch with a sigh after taking a sip of her wine.

"Tell me about it."

"How is Jordan doing?"

The trouble with best friends was that they were able to ask the hard questions.

"Much better," she said honestly though it wasn't clear if that gave Kate an idea. "It's been tough."

Kate nodded.

"But we're not going to let one bigoted individual keep us down. We have other things to do with our lives." Ellie cringed a bit at sounding like a social media motivational meme when those words did nothing to reflect her deepest, secret fears. "We've had good days and bad days. Lately, there have been many more good days. We're doing okay."

"I'm glad," Kate said softly.

Ellie was glad, too, even though some lingering concerns acted up every once in a while, like today, when she decided to pay Jordan a visit at work.

They had worked through the aftermath of the attack, in every possible way. They had talked all the implications to bits and pieces. Jordan was tired of talking about it, she had said so, and Ellie knew it was time to cut her some slack. There was nothing they could do to change what happened—the only way to go was forward. Ellie was usually all about forward.

"Thanks. Now let me hear what's new with you?"

Against all odds, they managed to stick to lighter subjects until Jordan returned, Derek in tow.

"I thought you might want a ride," he said to Kate who gave him a smile as she raised her glass.

"Good thinking. You'll drop me off here in the morning?"

"Sure."

"Tell me something good." Jordan sighed. "We spent the past few hours waiting on people, with few results. Victim's son is still AWOL. Autopsy results will take longer than expected, given the additional remains on the property."

"What about the witness?" Ellie asked.

"Not much there. The woman repeated her story verbatim, nothing much from her family except that Salter was a grumpy old man, and the kids didn't like him much. The boy thought he was creepy."

"Is it true that Sam fell through the floor?" Kate asked. "That must have been a shock."

"That, and the bones in that space."

"You think someone was held there?"

Kate might not be a cop any longer, but obviously she was still thinking like one. In the resulting awkward silence, she said, "Forget about it. You really don't want to hear my theories anymore. I'm sorry."

"No, it's a legit question," Jordan said. "We've been thinking about this. You have any left?" she asked pointing to the bottle.

"Sure. I'll get you a glass." Ellie jumped to her feet. She, too, was happy to end the conversation about someone possibly held against their will in a tight space—even though she might have to go back to it tomorrow. "By the way, Ariel called earlier. She's been training for a competition, and she was asking if we'd like to come watch this weekend. You could come, too," she said to Kate and Derek.

"Sure, I'd love to." Kate's response was swift. "She's pretty amazing."

The murder of a young woman by the Prophets of Better Days cult had been the last straw for Kate to leave the force. Ariel had made it out of the same cult, and she was thriving in her new life with her family, new friends and a curriculum that didn't prepare her to be a subservient wife.

Ellie thought it was strange how all their stories connected to this group, Kate's decision, her and Jordan's failed attempt at adopting Ariel. Kate had found a new career, and Ariel was happy living with her aunt. But the cult's long reach had come back to haunt them, in the form of a young woman who had chosen bigotry over freedom, regardless of the cost to her, her children, and others.

"That's settled, then."

She was aware of Jordan's gaze on her, concerned, probably a mirror image of her own. They had moved forward, but at times, recent experiences had left them raw, tiptoeing around

17

each other still. It would get better. This wasn't the first close call they'd survived.

Chapter Three

When Jordan came out of the bathroom the next morning, the bed was empty. Heading downstairs, she was surprised by the scents of pancakes and caramel. In the kitchen, the sight of Ellie wearing an apron over her nightgown gave her a rush of affection. Jordan couldn't help it. She stepped close behind her and leaned in to kiss her neck, content to feel her shiver.

"This looks great."

"Thanks, but don't get used to it on a weekday. It's probably going to be another long day. I wanted to make sure you don't sneak out of the house without breakfast."

"I didn't plan to, but the same goes for you. You'll come in later today?"

"After I drop Meri off at Jack and Pauline's, yes. Anything I should know?"

"Every day we don't get to talk to the son doesn't look that great for us, so it's likely going to be frustrating. There's something that's bothering me about Salter, and I'm not sure what it is."

"Well, the fact that there were bones in his basement? The Prophets had them too, and remember for what reason."

"Yeah, I was thinking about that too. We keep coming back to them, don't we?"

"I don't think there's a connection," Ellie said as she put a plate in front of Jordan. "There are too many women-hating creeps in the world."

"You keep saying that word...but I don't disagree." Jordan took a sip of her coffee and sighed in bliss. "I can't tell you how grateful I am. You've been doing a lot more than your share lately."

"We're a family. Making sure my wife gets fed before work is my share," Ellie said with a laugh.

Jordan studied her as if she wanted to say more on the subject, but she didn't. "Those are great," she said with regard to the pancakes. "I need to get going, see what Adams has for us on those bones."

"A few more minutes. They'll call you if there's anything important, right?"

"I sure hope so. All right. Give me another one?"

For some reason, this felt like victory to Ellie.

Sure enough, a phone call had lured her away from the cozy domestic scene, and after brushing her teeth, Jordan was on her way to the station, talking to Derek on the phone.

"It's good," he said without preamble. "Son just walked into the station. I thought you'd like to be here for this."

"You bet I would. And, finally. Has he said anything yet?"

"I got him settled with a coffee. Once you get here, we'll get started."

"Sounds great. Give me ten, and get me a coffee too?"

"Aren't you coming from breakfast?"

"So?"

He laughed. "I'll see you then."

Jordan hoped that Dr. Adams would have something to tell them as well. A quick solve, a case coming together early in the process, those were good signs. A few minutes later she walked into the station and went straight to the interrogation room where Derek was waiting with a man in his fifties who vaguely resembled Salter.

"Detective Carpenter," she said, shaking his hand. "Mr. Salter, I'm very sorry for your loss."

"Don't be," he said, surprising her. "No one is."

She exchanged a look with Derek before she sat. "Why would you say that?"

"You must know, he was a bitter old man, angry and spiteful at the world. He wasn't much of a father either, or a husband to my mother...but unlike me, she felt obliged to stay with him."

"You checked up on him every once in a while, the neighbor said?"

"Yeah, well, there was no lost love, but I wanted to make sure he wasn't dead. He wouldn't leave that house, and I didn't know what else to do."

Even though he denied it, perhaps Salter junior had felt some obligation after all. Jordan wondered if there was a deeper story behind the complicated relationship.

"I'm sorry I have to ask. You said he was angry. Was he ever abusive to you or your mother? Or anyone else that you were aware of?"

He snorted. "Verbally or physically? The answer is both. He believed in physical discipline, whatever that meant in his twisted mind, and I'm pretty sure he didn't stop at family. I left when I could, and I only came back when he knew better than to come at me."

"Mr. Salter, where were you three nights ago?" Derek asked.

He gave a wry laugh. "You have to ask that, right? I was traveling for work. I can show you some receipts."

"That would be helpful, thank you. Did your father ever mention any enemies, someone who had threatened him?"

"Only all unmarried women, gay people and immigrants in the world. You make of that what you want."

Jordan suppressed a groan. She would have given a lot to have this turn out to be a cut and dried murder case, the motive, passion or greed, whatever. They'd been dealing with far too many proud bigots lately. Chances were, before he became a victim himself, Charles Salter had hurt a lot of people, like his son, and his wife.

Yet, they had to find who killed him. The most obvious suspect was sitting right in front of them, though if Salter junior was to be believed, they had many other options.

"Anyone specific?" she asked.

"Hard to say. He was the type of person to start an argument with strangers if parents were okay with buying a doll for a boy. He wrote letters to the editors of newspapers on a regular basis."

"Did he have a computer?" They hadn't found any in the house.

"Not that I know of, but if that was the case, he certainly would have become one of those internet trolls."

"Mr. Salter, thank you for coming in. Please provide us with those receipts as soon as possible. If you can think of anything else, let us know."

"I'll do that."

Derek went to see him out. After he returned, his first words were, "That's a lot of anger."

"No kidding. Angry enough to hit him over the head with that branch multiple times?" Derek didn't answer, knowing that the question was rhetorical at this stage. "All right," she said, getting to her feet. "Let's see what Dr. Adams has for us."

"I have good news and bad news," Dr. Adams informed them when they went to see her in the morgue.

Jordan shrugged. "Good news first. It's not like we can avoid the rest, can we?"

"Not really. All right. It won't come as a surprise that Mr. Salter here was killed by several blows to the head. You have the murder weapon—blood and brains are all over one end of it."

Jordan refrained from tapping her fingers on a surface, waiting until anything sounded like actual news to her.

"But, lucky for you, the person who wielded the branch, held it tightly enough to break their own skin. There was an interesting amount of blood."

"That sounds promising," Derek agreed, and Dr. Adams gave him a smile.

Jordan was a bit more cautious about what was to come. "Please don't tell me that's all the good news you have."

"Think, Detective."

A few seconds later, she felt a tad embarrassed. "If you compare the two, you can probably guess if the killer and his victim were related."

Dr. Adams nodded. "We are pretty sure they aren't, though the size of the sample allows for some additional testing that might be helpful. Now, on to the bad news. I can't give you much on the bones yet. If I had to guess, I'd say they have probably been there a few years, but here's the thing: Not all of them belong to the same person."

Jordan stopped herself short of using a swear word. "Wait, there's more than one victim?"

"I believe that's what I just said. There are at least two males, from what I can tell. I don't know much more yet."

"We need to ID them. The son already suggested that Salter was abusive to everyone around him. If we find who these bones belonged to, we're likely to find who hated him enough to bludgeon him with that branch."

"I'll let you know when I know more," Dr. Adams said.

Outside the door, Derek said, "Damn, the son did look good to me. Picking up that branch, it looks pretty personal and spontaneous. It's not something a person would use if they plan ahead, like a knife...or a gun," he added quickly.

Jordan wasn't going to dwell on the personal connection to that subject, though the imagery made her wince.

"You're right. But I think we still need some more research on father and son to determine why those bones ended up in the cellar. If junior didn't do it, he could have known about it—his father's crimes, and that someone planned to avenge them."

"Let's keep that in mind. I'll go see Rogers," Derek said, referring to a Missing Persons detective they had worked with on several occasions. "There's another possibility as to why the two don't share DNA—if he wasn't Salter's biological son."

"It's a bit far-fetched, but at this stage, it's all possible. I'll talk to him again. Maybe I'm lucky. If he happens to be a murdering psychopath, they tend to open up to me."

"Yeah, I'm not sure if that's supposed to be funny. At least they're all dead or locked up, not that we can say for certain in the case of *former* detective Shriver."

"Don't say that name out loud," Jordan warned. "Ellie just barely got over the fact that you had to close that file."

"Neither of you has anything to worry about. There's no way he could have survived that jump."

He was aware that this wasn't much of a consolation for anyone. They would have preferred to see Shriver on trial and convicted for his crimes rather than dead after the stunt he'd pulled. It wasn't up to them.

"Let's meet for lunch later and pull everything together," she suggested.

"Sounds good to me. See you then."

Salter senior had started out as a factory worker and made it to foreman, staying within a certain radius for most of his life. He had bought the house over thirty years ago and lived there until his death.

As suspected, Jordan couldn't find any papers filed with the city regarding the addition. Had it been made when the need to hide a body first arose?

A few phone calls revealed that Salter junior had started out in the same company his father had retired from and went to college and a few semesters of medical school. After dropping out, he'd changed gears and found an entry level job in a medical research facility. That was still his occupation.

She found him arranging some papers, his colleague sending her a curious look when she greeted him.

"Detective Carpenter," he said. "I didn't expect to see you again so soon. Did you already find out who killed my father?" Judging by his tone, he could have just as well asked her about the weather. The co-worker's eyes widened, but he made no move.

"Could we talk somewhere in private?"

"I guess so. Could you finish up here meanwhile?" he addressed the younger man who looked disappointed. Salter led her out of the room and along a hallway, where he opened the door to an empty office.

"So, what is this all about?"

"There's no easy way to say it, but I have to ask. We found bones in your father's basement. We're currently working on identifying who these remains belonged to, but I wanted to check with you to see if you had any idea."

He gave a surprised, self-conscious laugh. "Why would I? Honestly, I'm beginning to think I should confer with a lawyer. For someone I talked to once every few years, my old man sure is giving me a lot of trouble. Bones? I assume it would be a family pet or something? We're not a *Psycho* type of family if that's what you were thinking. I can show you my mother's grave if you need that information."

"So, you have no idea?" Those bones were human without a doubt, so his words didn't hold much of a point—but it was possible that he didn't know.

"Not the slightest, I'm sorry. My father wasn't a good man, as I've told you before, but this...I don't see it. Maybe you should look at the previous owner, or there was actually a graveyard on the property at some point?" He shuddered. "Excuse me, now this is freaking me out a little."

"It is unsettling," she agreed. "Do you know when your father made the addition to the house? Did you help him with that, or do you know anyone who did?"

"Addition? No. I'm sorry I'm no help, but the house has been the way it is for as long as I can remember. Again, the previous owner might be able to help if they're still around."

"I'll look into that, thank you."

"You're welcome, Detective. Can I go back to work now?"

"Sure. Thanks for your time, Mr. Salter."

"Anything I can do to help. This...It's not very surprising that my father drew someone's ire, but it's all a nightmare nonetheless."

"I can imagine," she said.

⁂

"There are bones of two men, maybe more, in that basement, and Salter claims he had no idea." Jordan summed up their morning after they'd sat down for lunch in a coffee shop near the station. "How did it go with Rogers?"

"He has a few possible candidates for us, based on what Melissa said. She called me, by the way…She thinks the men were fairly young, early twenties at the most when they died."

"Maybe we're looking in the wrong place," Jordan wondered out loud. "The whole house was bound to fall down at some point. The structure is unsafe. They could have been curious and cocky, and gotten trapped? Ugh. What a way to die."

Derek looked doubtful.

"You think Salter wouldn't know if someone was in his basement?"

"Eric spent quite a bit of time trying to tell me the previous owner might have been implicated," she said. "A bit too much, for my liking, but what if they really didn't know about those bones?"

"Not likely. According to Melissa, they're not old enough."

"So, we believe Salter senior killed, or at the very least, allowed the deaths of two people?"

"Makes sense, doesn't it? A family member found out and came to confront him, Salter dismissed him and turned to go back into his house…and there was the conveniently located branch."

"It's looking more and more like that. I did as much research as I could without a warrant, and I didn't find anything suggesting Eric wasn't Mr. and Mrs. Salter's biological son." Jordan sighed and waved the waitress to their table for a coffee refill.

"Matching blood samples, that would have been too easy."

"Dr. Adams said she might be able to give us more with that sample," Derek reminded her. "And if they left this much blood on the murder weapon, where did it come from? It could be helpful to know."

"Yeah. I guess some more historical research is in order, too, to compile the long list of people Salter pissed off."

"Ellie is back today, isn't she? She loves that kind of thing."

"Yes, she does," Jordan said with a smile. "Good idea."

"Don't sound so surprised."

Chapter Four

E llie was more than happy to be brought up to speed on the case and dig into some of the research. She, too, had worked with Detective Rogers on a few occasions and knew him to be meticulous.

She had a list of names of young men aged seventeen to twenty-two who had gone missing in the area within the timeframe Dr. Adams had identified.

One of them had worked in the factory where Charles Salter had been foreman, but Salter was long retired at the time, and his son was no longer working there either. After going over all the files various times, this was still the only connection she could find.

Meanwhile, Jordan hung up her phone with a pensive expression.

"The previous owner is almost a hundred years old, no living relatives, but she claims no one in her family built that addition. So, we're back to the Salters."

"Walt Granger? Even if father or son wasn't working there anymore, they might have had friends or colleagues in common, some overlap?" Ellie suggested. "That's the only thing I have for now."

"It's something," Jordan agreed. "Let's check the others too, to be on the safe side."

In two cases, the parents who had reported their sons missing had either passed away or left the country.

Walt Granger's parents still lived in the city, and so did the sister of one of the missing persons.

Ellie was about ready to start calling for interviews, but Jordan shook her head.

"Not yet. I want to give Doc Adams a bit more time before we go to any of the loved ones. I know the connection to the Salters is important, but I also want to know if there was something they all had in common."

"A killer targeting and kidnapping young men, that's what you're thinking?" Derek asked. "Uncommon."

"But not unheard of. Let's do some more digging. If Dr. Adams can't come up with anything more specific, we can still see those families."

By the end of the day, it was clear that they'd have to set up those interviews. Dr. Adams confirmed that dental records had shown Walt Granger to be one of the bodies found in Salter's basement. That, and she'd distinguished a third victim from the bones unearthed. Lieutenant Carroll agreed that it was a good idea to take a closer look at all those recent cases.

If the general state of the world often made her want to lose all hope, Ariel's story, in addition to her own circle of family and friends, never failed to make Jordan feel a lot better about the possibilities. Ariel's statement against the Prophets of Better Days had been vital to hold the members of the cult accountable for their crimes. The list was long, and it ranged from murder, including that of Ariel's biological mother Deborah, rape and kidnapping to polygamy, tax fraud and illegal weapons deals. Ariel's courage had prompted other members to speak out.

Ariel had battled prejudice and threats from her "family" and the grief over her mother. She was thriving now, able to rely on those closest to her.

The idea of what could have been would always be bittersweet to Jordan and Ellie, but they were happy for Ariel to have the life she had with her aunt and teachers able to identify and nurture her talents. Now with access to training and coaching, she had a bright future ahead of her.

Even in this context, Jordan couldn't help thinking of the bones in the basement, Walt Granger and the others, and how they might have ended up there. Even with Ellie beside her, and Meri in her lap sleeping through the excitement of Ariel's achievements.

She watched Ariel talk to an older boy, the two of them smiling and hugging before she joined her teammates again.

Becca Crane, Ariel's aunt and adoptive mother wasn't here at the moment, but Jordan couldn't help wondering who he was—or if Becca knew about him. He, too, went to join a group closer to his own age.

Jordan hugged Meri a bit closer to her. There was no need to become paranoid. Of all people, Ariel knew the dangers of trusting too soon and too easily...Then again, she was a teenager. Jordan might give Becca a heads-up and gently raise the issue with Ariel.

At this moment, she was grateful she had made it through the week with this new case, identifying possible subjects and following leads. Things were truly back to normal, or at least she hoped they were.

The next morning, Dr. Adams joined them for the briefing as they discussed going forward. She and her team were still running tests on the blood sample.

"We're going to see Walt Granger's parents first thing today," Jordan said. "I don't want them to learn this from the press."

Lieutenant Carroll nodded. "Harding?"

"I found a Rosemary Hunt, Cooper Hunt's sister. She volunteers at a local homeless shelter, so I'm going to meet with her there. We'll see if there's any connection."

"Good. Let's hope we can bring this nightmare to an end soon."

Ellie caught Jordan's speculative gaze, wondering if they were thinking the same thing. This hope might be premature, but Carroll had to keep an optimistic attitude, for his team and his own superiors he had to answer to.

One by one, the detectives filed out of the room, off to their respective assignments. Ellie drove straight to the shelter where another volunteer pointed out Rosemary Hunt to her.

"Ms. Hunt. I'm Detective Harding. I'd like to talk to you about your brother Cooper."

The woman didn't seem much surprised. Nothing in her expression gave away any emotional reaction.

"Come with me, please," she said, leading them along a hallway into a cramped office. She pointed to the visitor's chair.

"Thank you."

"What would you like to know?" Hunt asked after she sat down. "My brother was a very private person. Is, I should say? I don't know. You must have an idea if you're here after all these years? You found out what happened to him?"

Cooper Hunt was a bit of an outlier, sixteen years since he disappeared at twenty years old, a college student. His older sister was calm, probably bracing herself for the worst possible news.

"We don't know for sure," Ellie admitted. "Do the names Charles Salter or Eric Salter mean anything to you?"

Rosemary frowned. "Should they? I'm not sure. Wait, wasn't that the man they found dead a few days ago? Why do you think Cooper would have anything to do with that?"

"No, we know that's not the case. Please, it could be helpful. Do you remember ever hearing these names before? The family lived in town for a long time."

"I don't know, I swear. Come to think of it, there might have been a Salter in the factory I worked at for a while."

"Did Cooper ever come to visit you at that job, or did he ever apply to work there?"

Rosemary Hunt looked baffled. "He asked around for a summer job once. He stayed for a few weeks but then found something else. It was the same year he disappeared. Oh God, you don't think...?"

Another connection with the Salters. If Charles wasn't responsible for the bodies in his basement, was it possible that someone from that former job of his had set him up?

"Ms. Hunt, I know it's been a long time, but do you remember who he spoke to, or if someone objected to him working there?"

"There was a co-worker talking behind his back, but we quickly shut that down. We were a close-knit group...and that co-worker is dead anyway. He was gossiping about everyone. I can't imagine he actually ever hurt anyone."

"Gossiping about what?"

"Cooper is gay."

"That was nowhere mentioned in the missing persons report," Ellie said.

"Yeah, I'm not surprised my parents didn't mention that."

"Do you know if he had a boyfriend at the time?"

"Cooper? I don't think so. He was just starting to figure things out for himself. I had hoped he'd be able to do so when he went away for college, but..." Her expression darkened. "It doesn't look that way, does it?"

Ellie couldn't disagree. She thought about Walt Granger, for certain a victim of the killer who had used Salter's basement to bury the bodies. Rogers was old enough to have been around for some of those cases. If there was a pattern, and loved ones had been less than forthcoming, would he have missed such a detail?

"I'm sorry," she said. "Thank you for your time, Ms. Hunt. We'll let you know if we find anything else."

She'd have to make some calls.

It was Walt Granger's father who started crying, placing the blame for his son's death in no uncertain terms.

"I always knew something bad would happen when he didn't want to give up the lifestyle."

"What lifestyle are you talking about?" Derek asked even though the answer was pretty clear. Granger's mother looked like she was angry at her husband. For a reason, Jordan thought, though nothing of this development surprised her much. The killer would choose victims he believed to be vulnerable. A member of a marginalized group facing a lack of support from close family members would qualify.

"The gay lifestyle, of course," Granger's father said as if surprised Derek had asked him that question. "They're all predators, and one of them preyed on my son!"

Jordan didn't think it would help to remind him that their number one suspect had been a man living with his wife and son. If Eric had told the truth, and Charles had acted as the abusive patriarch, it all made sense. On the bright side, and she was trying hard to find one in this mess, it could mean that they could close the cases on the missing men.

"Excuse me," she said when her phone rang, relieved she was able to avoid the toxic ideas in this room for a bit. She stepped outside on the porch, already breathing easier when she heard Ellie's voice. "Hey. What do you have?"

"A possible pattern," Ellie said.

"Let me guess. The 'gay lifestyle.' So far, there's nothing to deter me from the idea that Mr. Salter senior could be a serial killer targeting young men who faced difficulties at home."

"To put it mildly," Ellie agreed. "Three that we know of…There could be more, right?" she asked after a moment of hesitation.

"Aren't there always?" Jordan sighed. "Let's focus on the ones we have. Any other news?"

"I talked to Rogers. He wasn't able to connect the cases at the time, but he agrees it's worth taking a look with the information from Hunt's sister…and you are sort of confirming my theory."

"Let me and Derek finish up here, and we'll meet you at the station?"

"I'll be there," Ellie said.

⌒⌒

"Let me get this straight," Lieutenant Carroll said when they were back at the station to bring together their findings. "We've gone from a man being murdered in the woods around his house to a serial killer targeting young gay men, and we have no idea yet how many victims there could be?"

Jordan had to admit he wasn't wrong. "We are working close-ly with Missing Persons to identify all the victims from the basement. The pattern seems fairly obvious. If we're lucky and the killer stuck to one location, this could be the end of it. Our team is still out there though. Silver lining—a dead serial killer."

"Who died under yet unclear circumstances. If there's some-one out for vigilante justice, I want to know that too."

"We're working on it," Jordan confirmed. "My money's not on Walt Granger's parents. They're still grappling with the fact he was gay...they seem to be honestly grieving, but I can't see them confront Salter. Ellie?"

Ellie had drifted a bit, admiring how Jordan was handling her return to a full-on case load. It was the way she'd always dealt, throwing herself into work. There was no need to question a functioning method. Even though she was here at the table, a detective herself, the admiration that drew her to Jordan early on would always linger...

"Yes! Rosemary Hunt, Cooper Hunt's sister..." Ellie sat up straighter, focused on the matter at hand now. "She knew he was gay, but she didn't seem to have much of an opinion either way. She doesn't strike me as a vigilante either. None of the other men had any obvious connection to Salter."

"Eric Salter hinted that his father harbored bigoted attitudes. No one but Charles Salter has lived in that house in many years, and the remains of at least three victims were on the property." Jordan shrugged. "That looks pretty cut and dried to me. The only question is how many families can we give closure with this?"

Ellie noted that she sounded a bit testy. "I agree," she said, wondering if Jordan had heard something else. "As for the per-son behind the murder, we have that blood sample at least."

"Nothing to compare it to, yet," Derek added. "For that, in addition to the bones, we'll have to wait."

"I'm aware. I appreciate the update, now get back to work."

By the end of their shift, they had found out that another of the missing men had identified as gay, one as bi. A lot of information to process, even though some of the pieces were still missing when they left the station that night.

Jordan was silent as they walked along the hallway to the front door.

"Not such a bad week, right?" Ellie began.

Jordan stopped, as if surprised by her statement, and since they were alone in the hallway, Ellie used that moment to embrace her from behind. "Things are moving. We might have figured this out by the end of next week."

"Yeah. Sure. What are you getting at?"

Ellie suppressed a sigh. She wasn't about to go against what she'd discussed with Kate. She knew she had to keep her own worries in check, and that was on her.

"Come on," Jordan, who had guessed what was on her mind, said. She turned to Ellie. "I'm fine. I have been for a while, and yes, you taking care of Meri for those days helped. It sucks that there are a lot of proud bigots in the world, but we're not going back to that again. I'm happy to be working. I got over it."

That was a lot more of an answer than Ellie had asked for. It sounded reasonable to her.

"Yes, you're right. I'm sorry. I didn't mean to suggest otherwise."

"I understand. This is like the Prophets all over again, except no one's wrapping it into their sick idea of religion. If we're right about Salter, sick is all there is."

They started walking again.

"Thank God for decent people," Ellie said. "Speaking of which, why don't we call Pauline, and all have dinner at the *SEVEN*?" The bar run by Jordan's parents was by far more than their new favorite hangout.

"Good idea. Then we can relieve Mom of babysitting duties earlier, and we'll take Meri home with us afterwards," Jordan reasoned. "Let's do it." Her cell phone rang. "All right, hold that thought." Dr. Melissa Adams was on the other end. Jordan put her on speaker.

"I'm about to leave the building. Are you going to make me change my mind?"

"That depends," Dr. Adams said. She always seemed to sound a tad cheerful for the work she was doing. "Your team over at Salter's house finished up today, which means I could finish sorting those bones. I got some more news. Three victims that we could cross-reference with your list of missing persons, five overall."

Jordan winced. "That's a serial killer all right. Anything to tie Salter to them?"

"Not really, but I found something interesting about that other blood sample. They must have been bleeding heavily, but it's lucky for us. We had an amount big enough to figure out that person was on various heavy medications."

"Hallucinogens?" Ellie asked. "Hi, Doc."

"Detective Harding. No, I mean more along the lines of pain medication, and prolonged exposure. Most of us could not walk upright with these doses, let alone beat someone to death with a branch."

"That is curious indeed," Jordan admitted. "Send everything to me, please, and I'll take a look first thing in the morning."

"Not in a hurry to find out who killed the killer, are we?"

"I'm in a hurry to get home to my daughter."

"I wasn't implying anything. I'm sending you everything this minute. Enjoy your evening."

"I will, thanks."

"Do you want to go back?" Ellie asked just to make sure. "We could take a look...?"

"Tomorrow," Jordan decided. "Whoever picked up that branch targeted Salter senior. That means they're unlikely to kill anyone else, especially if they're as doped up as she says they are."

Ellie shrugged. "Fine with me. Let's go."

Chapter Five

T he *SEVEN* had been built on the grounds of the popular cop bar *Code Seven* by Jack Carpenter and friends of his. Currently, it often served as a home base for Jordan and Ellie. They could bring Meri there, have dinner in a quieter corner and still spend time with their friends.

Sam Potts was still on sick leave. There wasn't much she could do at work with her right hand in a cast, but she, too, joined them for an hour.

"I'm just staring at the walls anyway, and this way I get to see the cutest baby in town."

Meri gave a broad smile as if aware of the compliment, causing everyone to laugh.

"Isn't that the reason we're all here?" Casey, her T.O., alleged. "I was sure I didn't want to go there again, but she's testing my resistance. I could imagine having another little one in the house..."

Jordan couldn't help thinking how lucky they were, and how, thanks to a well-functioning support system, they'd been able to handle all the recent changes. She didn't want to think of a time before Ellie and Meri in her life.

She was grateful that no one was mentioning Joy Anne Deane any longer, not even with this case that bore surprising similarities. Or perhaps it wasn't surprising, because bigotry translated into crime a lot more often than people thought, because for too long, toxic attitudes had been indulged. But this wasn't just about attitudes—Charles Salter, if he was the killer, had been a predator. Someone had stopped him, but what was the real motive?

Ellie knew her better than anyone. She should have gone back to check Dr. Adams' email.

⌐

Derek and Kate had joined them as well as Maria Doss and her girlfriend, A.D.A. Valerie Esposito. Seeing that Meri was starting to fuss in her highchair, Jordan commented, "I think it's time to call it a night." She got up for one last trip to the restroom, her mind still on Salter, his alleged crimes and the heavily medicated perpetrator. Opening the door, she flinched at the image of Sam cowering in the corner, crying.

Jordan locked behind herself and crouched in front of her distraught colleague.

"Hey. Sam. What's going on?" Her injury had to be frustrating, but it was in no way life-threatening. "It's okay, I'm here. Breathe, slowly."

The seconds ticked by as Sam's breathing became calmer, and her gaze more focused. Jordan cautiously reached out to touch her shoulder, pushing her own mixed emotions aside for the moment. "That's it. You're okay."

"Wow." Sam ran a trembling hand over her face. She looked embarrassed but let Jordan help her to her feet.

"We can drive you home," Jordan said, waiting as Sam washed her hands and face. "You know what brought this on?" She had an idea, the imagery hitting uncomfortably close to home.

"I think we know what brought this on," Sam said, sounding frustrated. "I've been keeping it together pretty well but falling through the floor and being trapped in a small space wasn't helpful."

Jordan remembered how she'd acted unfazed in the situation. But those moments had a way of staying with a person. She knew all about it.

"It's not about the small space at all."

"No, it's not. I still think he got off easy."

It was a hard truth for either of them that the man who had assaulted Sam had once been a cop—and that a handful of his old friends still thought he shouldn't have lost the job over it.

"He did. Atwood still giving you trouble?"

Chris Atwood was one of the officers who had stood by Cliff Waters.

Sam shook her head. "He barely talks to me when we work together, and that's fine with me. I'm sorry. It's none of your concern."

"You're a friend, so it's definitely our concern," Jordan disagreed. "How about that ride?"

"I'd appreciate it. Jordan...?"

Her hand already on the handle, Jordan turned around, wondering why, within a heartbeat, she'd become the one to feel claustrophobic.

"How did you get over it? He was by far worse than Cliff."

Talk about claustrophobic places. "There's a reason why we don't compare trauma. It's not a competition." She was wondering if Sam was giving her too much credit, and if she really had any wisdom to share with her younger colleague. "You take it one day at a time. Remind yourself you're still here and focus on yourself, and your career."

"I admire you," Sam said. "And Ellie. You've been through so much, and you still do the job everyday and you're there for your friends and family."

"And you are the same. I swear. Now let's go find Ellie and Meri."

"Let's do that. Thank you." Sam's small smile told her she was well aware of how Jordan handled the unexpected praise.

❧

Jordan didn't get to take a look at Dr. Adams' findings right away, because she got two phone calls, one of which had the potential to change the trajectory of the case.

The first one came from Eric Salter.

"I thought you should know this...I'm not sure if it's important, but my father was very interested in college sports. He sometimes bet on local teams in bars...I don't know, there might be a connection, and he made someone angry, failed to pay a debt?"

"Thank you, Mr. Salter. We're going to look into this."

She was about to open the email from Dr. Adams, when her phone rang again.

"Detective Carpenter, how can I help you?"

"Hello, I'm Detective Ann McCoy. I was hoping I could take a few minutes of your time."

"What is this about?" She didn't really have that much time, but after the woman told her where she was calling from, Jordan was intrigued.

"This might be a little far-fetched," McCoy admitted. "I was reading about a couple of your cases, and something stood out to me. Oliver Boyd, the kid who supposedly jumped off a cliff, and the bodies recently found in a house in the woods. Have you looked at a possible connection?"

Jordan sat up straight when the detective mentioned Boyd. He hadn't exactly gone missing but left his companions during a camping trip. His body had been found at the bottom of a cliff, and she couldn't remember anything that might have tied him to Salter. He, too, was gay. Coincidence? He had spent part of the night with a man yet to be identified. But that couldn't have been Salter.

"So far, what we have are several young gay men who were reported missing, their bones found in a murder victim's basement. We couldn't prove any foul play in Boyd's case, and he doesn't fit the profile one hundred percent. The other victims had no one to turn to and were dealing with a toxic, homophobic environment. Oliver Boyd's parents were supportive. There was some conflict with a friend though. Why are you asking?"

"I hate to say it, but there might be another one. A young college student. We thought he might have left on his own, but his story fits. There was definitely a toxic environment."

Jordan was overly aware of the chill running down her spine. Detective McCoy sounded as if she was already sure that the missing college student, Boyd and the victims in Salter's basement were connected. If that was the case, what did it mean? Had they made a mistake with Salter—or was there already a copycat, and he might have killed Salter in order to take out the competition?

"I'm listening," she said.

Two steps into the break room, Ellie almost walked out backwards. The fridge was pulled back, and she saw various tools on the floor.

"The vending machine is still working," a voice called from behind it, and a moment later, Ellie came face to face with the employee from the repair service.

"Thanks. A coffee is all I need."

"Please, go ahead. I'm almost done here."

"Big job?"

"Not that big. You really want to hear more about it?" the woman asked.

"Not really." Ellie laughed and turned to the vending machine. She was well aware that the younger woman was giving her the eye, and she found it both amusing and flattering.

"Yeah, it's not that thrilling. I bet your job is."

"It can be," Ellie said, wondering if Jordan would want her to bring her a chocolate bar. Probably. "But we'll be grateful to have a functioning fridge again."

"Glad to be of service. I'm Izzy, by the way."

"Well, have a good day, Izzy...Hey. Jordan. You're here." Ellie jumped a little when Jordan walked inside.

"I am. Are you getting anything?"

"Yes, I was thinking coffee and snacks. I think we might need them." The past few days, she had diligently added names and cases to the board.

"I agree. I have news too," Jordan said, casting a quick glance at Izzy who listened with interest. She walked over to the vending machine and started feeding it coins. After they'd both picked up their purchases and left the room, Jordan commented,

"The repair lady is quite fond of you."

"Is she? It's a good thing I'm happily married, and my wife isn't jealous at all," Ellie returned, making her laugh as they walked to the briefing room.

"She's not. She knows she doesn't have reason to be."

"True. She's also extremely modest," Ellie teased.

They both sobered up when they entered the room where not only the board had expanded, but also the number of attendees. Detective Rogers stood in a corner with Lieutenant Carroll. They both took a seat when Jordan and Ellie walked in. Detectives Henderson and Doss were present as well, and so was Sergeant Bristol.

"Okay, this is where we are," Ellie said when she had everyone's attention. She pointed to the board. "It starts with the remains found in Charles Salter's house. The bodies we identified." She walked to the other side. "Missing Persons cases that fit the profile."

"Please tell me we're talking theory at this point," Lieutenant Carroll said, looking dismayed.

What did he expect? "Well, that's how we usually start." Carroll's raised eyebrow and her colleagues' barely suppressed chuckles told Ellie her comment might have been a bit too much tongue-in-cheek. She cleared her throat. "Okay, as marked here, some of them have a connection to the factory where Salter worked. Plus, apparently, he had a thing for local college sports. We've been looking into the possibility of gambling debts, but it seems more likely that this is where he found his victims."

"And we assume he targeted gay men?"

"That's the pattern we've seen emerging." Ellie was aware of the heavy atmosphere in the room.

"What about Salter's murderer?" Carroll asked. "Carpenter?"

"I have something to add to that as well," Jordan said. "But as to your question, we're looking for someone who's on heavy medication. We should be able to narrow it down soon, because you can't get that particular kind over the counter. I expect us to know more within the next forty-eight hours or so. And...A detective from out of town contacted me. She's working on a case where a young gay man recently went missing. I called Salter back, and he told me that his family sometimes took vacations in that area, though he doesn't know if his father went lately."

"We're still looking at murders he might have committed before his death, or an admirer-slash-copycat?" Maria asked.

"If we're lucky, it's the former. But she got me wondering if Oliver Boyd fit the pattern."

"No, come on, we've been over this." Ellie was surprised at Derek's swift and firm denial. Maybe that other investigator had a point, offering a different perspective? She knew Jordan had a hard time accepting the loose ends in this case, especially since it had been her first since the attack. "Boyd was a different story. Suicide."

"We never identified the other man he saw that night," Jordan insisted.

"It couldn't have been Salter. He's not exactly the demographic."

Jordan didn't look to happy, but she couldn't argue with the assessment. Besides, if there was another murderer, they had an even bigger problem.

"In any case, Detective McCoy will get back to me if she has anything new."

"Good," Carroll said. "I'd still prefer if it ends there, and you can find me the heavily medicated suspect soon. Let me know what you find out."

Sergeant Bristol got to his feet.

"Detective Harding, you'll come to roll call tonight? We need to get out the names of those on the board that haven't been identified yet. Some of them are recent. They could still be alive."

She nodded. "Let's hope we can rule them out as Salter's victims."

Chapter Six

Jordan and Derek stayed behind, studying the board some more.

Jordan's amusement at the repairwoman flirting with Ellie had quickly dissipated with the meeting. For a while, she'd worried that she might have had a lapse in judgment with the Boyd case. But Detective McCoy knew nothing about her state of mind, and she thought that there could be a connection between this case, hers, and the murders.

Who was right?

There was no good hopeful outcome in this. Oliver Boyd had either killed himself, or he'd fallen victim to a bigoted serial killer.

"Don't you hate the job sometimes?"

She didn't expect a conclusive answer from Derek Henderson, who gave her question some thought, nonetheless.

"I still hope that we can wrap this up fairly soon. There can hardly be any doubt that Salter committed the murders. The person who killed him seems to have severe health problems. If they get a good lawyer, they might never see the inside of a prison, and to be honest, I can live with that."

"Doesn't it bother you to think we might have gotten it wrong?"

"Sure, but what do you prefer? Going back to Mr. and Mrs. Boyd and tell them there's a small chance their son didn't die from suicide, but at the hands of a homophobic killer? That's going to make them feel better."

Knowing he was right didn't make it any easier.

"The name Detective McCoy gave me is Tim Caplan," she said. "Let's add him to the board for now."

It was perhaps dangerous for him to be here, but the police had a prime suspect. He could coast on that for a while. The more research he did, the more he knew he had found the perfect prey once again.

Unsupportive parents. Recent conflict with friends. His chosen subject was a promising athlete, but he'd been lacking lately, due to conflicts at home and in school. Wasn't his fault really, but...Too bad. It made him all the more interesting.

He also noticed that the small family was back, the two cops and the baby. He'd done his best to avoid them and stay closer to bigger groups of friends. He had to move soon before he blew his chances altogether.

The girl he'd seen with them the other day was back as well. He frowned as he watched her walk down from the bleachers to talk to his target, the two of them sharing a shy smile.

This wasn't good. She was in the way.

Jordan and Ellie had taken Ariel to dinner after her practice, along with Meri. When Ellie took their daughter to the bathroom, Jordan thought it was a good moment to address Ariel's obvious affection for the older boy she'd once again talked to earlier.

It turned out that Ariel had something to tell her too.

"I've been wanting to talk to you about this..." she began. "I hope you won't be too disappointed."

"No way. Whatever it is, you can tell me...us."

"Okay then. I thought it would be important, but I've been so busy with school and sports, and...It might be selfish, but I don't want to write that book anymore."

"That's it?"

"Yes. I've been thinking about it for a while."

"It has nothing to do with being selfish," Jordan affirmed. "You have helped the police, and with that, the girls in the cult, more than anyone else. There's nothing you owe to anyone."

"Thanks." She sighed in relief. "I wanted to talk to you first. I'm glad you understand."

"Ellie does, too, I promise you."

"Ellie always finishes things she starts, doesn't she?" Ariel said ruefully.

"True—but she wouldn't want you to give yourself so much pressure. I think Jennifer Beaumont's mother is working with a writer to get the story out as well, so...It's not all on you."

"I'm glad. There was something you wanted to tell me?"

Considering Ariel made grown-up decisions like that, Jordan might be getting ahead of herself, but she didn't want to take any chances.

"So, there's a boy you like?"

Ariel started laughing.

"Is that a funny question?"

"It kind of is. Remember, if I was still with the Prophets, I'd be married right now. No, thanks, I'm pretty happy to spend time with my family and friends. I'm not interested in anything else."

Jordan couldn't detect any hints that Ariel was lying. That gave her hope for the time they'd have to have a similar talk with Meri.

"The guy you talk to after training? He seems a bit older than you. Is he a friend?"

"Oh, you mean Owen! Yes, he's a friend." Realizing that Jordan was waiting for a bit more of an explanation, Ariel added, "And he's not interested in me that way, I swear. He's gay. One day, we started talking...He knew a bit about my story—of course, everyone does. He told me about his family. I guess we can both relate to feeling different and out of place."

"You feel out of place?"

Ariel shrugged. "It's no big deal. Sometimes, it's like that time was all one big bad dream...but my mom is gone. It's not the same for him. His parents are pretty mean, and his friends can't relate. We've been going for pizza or ice cream, and yes, Aunt Becca knows about it. She knows the family too."

"Okay. I may have overstepped. I'm sorry, but he seems like a good friend."

"He is. And don't worry. Aunt Becca had the same questions at first."

"What questions?" Ellie, who had returned to the table with Meri, asked.

"I guess you have to tell the story one more time."

"I don't mind. I'm really glad Becca and you guys listen."

Jordan thought of Tim Caplan whose story had sounded too much like Owen's. Perhaps it wasn't too much of an exaggeration to think this case was getting to her. But she was going to make sure they'd find the truth, for those young men. If their families didn't care, they had to show them that someone still did. She and Ellie, and their team did. Detective McCoy did. They were going to close these cases.

Back in his hometown, an eyewitness had reported Tim getting into a car with an older man, though they couldn't give much of a description—of the man or the car.

A trucker notified them that he'd picked up Caplan, who had been hitchhiking, and dropped him off at the nearest rest stop.

The next time Jordan spoke to Detective McCoy, the latter suggested she'd talk to her boss and come meet with them.

Jordan had no objections—the more eyes on this, the sooner they could close the case, and determine which names on the board belonged to Salter's case. She hoped that they might find out Caplan had simply run away to escape the pressure from his conservative parents. They could be lucky, right?

The more this case widened, the more likely that they'd have to call in the FBI.

Meanwhile, as she'd expected, they had a lead on the perp's medication. After excluding a man who had since been deceased, a pre-teen, and a woman who was wheelchair-bound in her home, there were two more men. Both of them were fathers, one a retired coach, the other the former owner of a business next to the factory Salter had worked for.

Jordan didn't have a good feeling when they went to the business owner's house to have a woman wearing black opening the door to them. It was a short visit after the widow described her late husband's condition.

They found the retired coach, Allan Cordell, at his home, doing dishes. He asked them to come in. He was moving slowly, using a cane.

Jordan and Derek shared a look. So far, it didn't seem like any of the persons taking this particular medication would be able to kill someone in the way that had led to Salter's death. She didn't believe that someone in the lab had made a mistake, but she'd have to double-check with Dr. Adams. A.D.A. Esposito wouldn't be amused if she'd gotten them the warrants based on faulty information. Perhaps she'd have to warn her too.

"Have a seat," Cordell said. "What do you want to know?" He still had gloves on and kept the dish towel in his hand.

"Does the name Charles Salter ring a bell?" Derek began.

Jordan studied the man closely for a reaction. It wasn't an emotional one.

"Salter, yes, sure, he was found dead recently. You're not supposed to speak ill of the dead, but man, he wasn't a good guy."

"Why do you say that?"

"Everyone knew that he was beating his son and his wife, and he had a lot of opinions on other people's lives. You wonder why the neighbor's house was empty for so long? No one wanted to live there. The poor family that moved in, they had no idea."

"You knew where he lived?"

"Everyone who met Salter, knew where he lived. Some kids would head out there and sneak around the house for a dare."

"Some kids?" Jordan echoed. "You have names?"

"Well, most of them are adults now and left town. Salter has been haunting the woods for some time."

"You have reason to assume he might have committed a crime?"

"Other than what I told you? I don't know. The wife is gone, and I think the son still comes to town every once in a while. Perhaps he's going to live in that house now, who knows."

Jordan perched on the edge of her seat. "Mr. Cordell, perhaps you can help us out here. Mr. Salter was beaten to death with a branch. We were able to get a blood sample from the person holding that branch, and it turns out they were on a specific kind of medication. The same that's part of your treatment."

"What?"

"Would you be willing to submit to a DNA test?"

"That's what this is about?" He shook his head in disbelief. "Of course I would, tell me when and where. If you did your research, you know that I barely leave the house, let alone at night. I can't drive because of that medication. How would I sneak out and kill somebody? I didn't like Salter, that's all."

"We could drive you to the station right now, if that's okay with you," Derek suggested. "You might want to have legal representation."

"Is that a fancy way of saying you're going to arrest me?"

"No, this is just for the DNA test."

"Well, I don't need a lawyer. I didn't do anything. You'll be able to clear that up in no time."

"All right then." Jordan got to her feet. "Let's go."

She watched as he peeled off the gloves, revealing scratches and bruises on his hands and wrists.

Cordell shook his head. "I don't know what you're thinking, Detective, but the only fight I've been in is with my disease, and my medication."

She wondered about his choice of words. Even if there hadn't been much of a fight involved in Salter senior's death, he might be trying to distract them. He still might have been the one who held that branch.

Derek had offered to bring Cordell back to his home. While waiting for his return, Jordan decided to make a brief stop at the A.D.A.'s office to bring her up to date.

Valerie Esposito shrugged when confronted with the latest development. "It doesn't look like anyone's going to sue, at least. It was a lead worth following. You're doing okay in all this?"

"Why wouldn't I?" Jordan asked, aware of her irritation. "I don't flinch every time I meet a bigoted criminal. There are too damn many of them."

"Can't argue with that. A case like that, it raises alarm bells. But at least you were able to give some families closure."

"Yeah. Whatever they'll do with that."

"That sounds ominous."

"I don't know. Some of them seem to have done whatever they could to push their kids away."

"Doesn't mean they deserve to lose them this way...or any other way," Valerie pointed out.

"You're right," Jordan relented. "I'm tired. Maybe I should call it a day."

"You do that but perhaps check with the ME first and let me know if there's anything else I need to know about."

"I will. Let's keep our fingers crossed."

Chapter Seven

D erek hadn't returned yet when Jordan sat down behind her desk and spent a few minutes shuffling her notes back and forth. Detective McCoy would arrive tomorrow. They were making progress. Even if Cordell didn't turn out to be their suspect, it was only a detour. A good night's sleep would make a difference. Start fresh.

She was allowed to be tired. It didn't mean she was going backwards. Ariel's revelations, Caplan's story, Salter's motive, it was draining, but yet, she was still here. She had survived the attack, was back on the job while she and Ellie were raising a child. She had a lot of good to counter the bad.

They had to wait on the DNA test, on what Detective McCoy could tell them. When her phone rang and the caller ID showed Ellie, Jordan decided to tell her she was going home for the day. Perhaps Ellie could too, though that wasn't a given.

"Hey." Ellie sounded apologetic for some reason. "Derek is already on his way, but I guess you'll want to come too."

"What happened?"

"You remember Mrs. Miller, Salter's neighbor?"

At this point, Jordan was certain that this wasn't news she'd be happy to hear. "Of course, is she okay?"

"Not really. They found a body on their property."

"A body. Bones, like in Salter's basement?"

"No. A fairly fresh grave."

Now Jordan understood the reason for Ellie's tone of voice. "Damn."

"Yes. That means Salter couldn't have done it."

"Any ID on the victim?"

"Not yet, but it should be quick. I don't think it happened more than forty-eight hours ago."

Jordan suppressed another curse. "I'm on my way," she said.

⁂

"Mrs. Miller, I'm really sorry. What happened?" She had made it before Derek. In the Millers' living room, they were crowded by the officers first on the scene, Marshall and Martin, and the crime scene unit.

Ellie sat on the couch with Mrs. Miller who jumped to her feet when she saw Jordan.

"Oh my God, this is a nightmare," she said, her eyes welling up for what probably wasn't the first time.

"I don't know any other way to describe it." Mr. Miller was coming down the stairs, resignation in his expression. "I thought it was better to have the kids upstairs for now."

"We'll have to talk to them too," Ellie reminded him softly.

"Yes, of course," he said with a shrug. "Give them a minute, will you?"

"We were away for a short trip," Mrs. Miller explained. "Just a couple of days, and...when we came back, we let our dog out to play in the backyard." She shuddered. "All of a sudden he started digging somewhere close to the border of our property—"

She didn't finish her sentence. Jordan got the picture.

"I noticed something wasn't right," Mr. Miller added. "It looked strange, nothing that we had done, so I got the kids inside and we took a closer look." He, too, was pale. "When we realized what that was, we called the police."

"Did you ask anyone to look after the house while you were gone? Someone might have seen something."

Mr. Miller shook his head. "It was only a couple of days, and we had the dog with us. No. With Salter dead, there's no one around here."

Except a killer who had left a body on the property of the woman who had found Salter. Coincidence? More like a sick sense of humor, Jordan thought. She caught Ellie's pensive gaze.

"Mr. and Mrs. Miller, I'm afraid this will take some time. I'll check with my colleagues, but it would be a good idea to take your family elsewhere for a few days."

"A few days?" Mr. Miller echoed. "What else are you expecting to find?"

Jordan listened closely. While they had put the emphasis on finding the missing men, not much had been said in the press on the subject of the bones in Salter's basement.

"Again, I'm sorry."

She went outside to inspect the gravesite illuminated by huge spotlights, where Dr. Adams and her team were at work.

"And I thought tonight would be an early night for *me*," Melissa greeted her.

"Yeah, that's not going to happen for either of us."

"I don't think so. Caucasian male, early twenties, body's been here for two, three days at the most."

The implications of those words were giving her a headache. Ellie had been right. Two or three days. That meant they were definitely looking at another killer. There were too many connections between Salter, the factory, and the previous victims not to assume he'd been responsible for the bones in the basement. Salter couldn't have buried this body, because someone had already killed him. Who? And was the same person responsible for this most recent crime?

She was tired all right.

"The Millers want to know if they can leave town." She jumped a bit at Ellie's voice behind her. "I told them it would be better if they were available."

"That's good. We still might have some questions after this is done."

"That's not Tim Caplan," Ellie said.

"No. Good news for Detective McCoy and his family, at least."

"In fact, I'm not sure he's on the board." Ellie appeared disturbed, and her words clearly conveyed the reason. "Oh my God, you don't think there are more bodies? This is starting to look like a horror movie."

"I'm not sure what I'm thinking," Jordan said grimly. She lowered her voice so only Ellie could hear. "We have to ID the victim, but meanwhile, could you look into the Millers some more? I'm sure they are innocent in this, but I want to know why someone chose their backyard for the burial site. Can't be just for convenience. There are endless possibilities out here."

"Sure, I can do that."

"Good. I'll wrap up here meanwhile. Derek should be here any minute."

She breathed a sigh of relief when Ellie had left. Jordan wasn't sure why, and she didn't want to examine the question too closely.

By the time they both came home, exhausted and not much the wiser, Meri was fed and sleeping soundly in her bed. Pauline sat on the couch with a paperback.

"I'm so sorry," Ellie said, suppressing a yawn. "I promise you, eventually we'll find a solution."

"Don't worry about it." Pauline closed her book. "She's the most amazing little girl. Have you eaten yet?"

With the new developments, she didn't even have time to think about it, but now Ellie felt almost nauseated with hunger.

"We'll order in something quick."

"You don't have to. I brought some food over. You just have to re-heat it."

"You're a lifesaver, thank you!" Jordan hugged her mother. "You'd like to stay?"

"Oh no, I'll meet Jack at the bar. Have a good evening. And I mean it, I love to spend time with my granddaughter, so don't hesitate to call."

When she had left, Jordan slumped on the couch. "This is freaky Friday. My parents are going to hang out at a bar, their bar, and I can barely keep my eyes open."

"Let's eat something, and we'll try to get some sleep," Ellie suggested.

"Yeah. Sounds like a plan."

She went to set the table while Ellie inspected the fridge and took out a couple of containers. She couldn't help thinking how privileged they were, having people like Jack and Pauline in their lives. Not every family was supportive, and the lack of a healthy environment created vulnerability. Something a predator could smell.

She put a bottle of water on the table and poured a glass of white wine for each of them.

"So, not much on the Miller family," she said. "Moderate conservative background, no connection to any of the victims so far, the only connection to Salter was that they were neighbors. Latest victim was not on our list, and we don't even know if he fit the pattern."

"He might have gone missing recently," Jordan reminded her. "All of this happened after Salter's death. That's bothering me. The other guy, was he working with Salter? Admiring him? Wanting to set him up? All those open questions, and we didn't even get to say goodnight to Meri. Sometimes I have doubts it's all worth it."

Ellie managed not to flinch. Being back on the job had been good for Jordan, her confidence and overall well-being, but lately, she kept dropping those small hints. Ellie wanted to convey that she was open to a conversation, whatever direction it might go in. At the same time, she knew now might not be a good moment, when they were both tired and stressed given the growing number of victims.

"I think we all do sometimes. Tomorrow will be better," she said. "That other detective, McCoy, might bring in a fresh perspective. And we'll find a way to have some family time, I promise."

Jordan acknowledged her ever hopeful point of view with a smile. It was all Ellie wanted.

❦

When Jordan sat down at her desk the next morning, Detective McCoy hadn't arrived yet, but they had an ID on the victim. Jordan stared at the picture of a younger Ashton Mayfield, thinking his smile looked forced. Whatever had troubled him, there was no chance of resolving any of it now, because at twenty-two, he was dead.

Since the age of fifteen, Mayfield had lived with an aunt who had since been deceased. One arrest for drug possession at eighteen, he'd gotten away with probation and community service and stayed under the radar ever since.

"You ready?" Derek asked, already in his coat, keys in hand.

The alarm had rung early, so they could have breakfast together before Pauline arrived—and a little too early for Meri who had been cranky the whole time. Unlike her moms, she was able to take a nap. Jordan aborted her train of thought, guiltily admitting that she was jealous of her baby.

"Sure. Let's go."

Ashton Mayfield's parents still lived in town, in a tidy suburban neighborhood, a park with a playground across the street.

Jordan leaned back in her seat with a sigh as Derek parked the car alongside the curb.

"You know, I've always hated this part. Everyone does, sure, but we're about to tell them someone decided to murder their child, very likely because of who he was."

"Yeah." Derek didn't argue with either one of her points. "You want to wait out here?"

Jordan cast another look at her phone. Nothing from McCoy. She really wanted to, but at the same time, she felt like her colleagues, maybe Derek in particular, were still watching her. In fact, they might have never stopped. The idea was disconcerting.

"No. Let's get this over with."

Mrs. Mayfield didn't seem surprised when they identified themselves to her, something Jordan found odd. She braced herself for tears, and worse.

"Mrs. Mayfield, is your husband home?" She probably wouldn't suspect the question to have a sexist subtext, and it didn't. If they could get both of them in the same room, this would be over sooner.

"No, but you can talk to me." Ashton's mother was in her fifties, though she looked older. "Come on in. This is about Ashton, right? Was it drugs, or did he have a disease?" She kept talking as she walked ahead of them into the living room. Behind her back, Jordan and Derek exchanged a quizzical look.

Mrs. Mayfield was probably in shock, bracing herself for what she was about to hear.

"I'm so sorry," Jordan said. "Your son was murdered."

That got a minute reaction from the woman, her eyes widening a fraction.

"Murdered? How?"

The lack of emotion in the woman's reaction felt unnerving to Jordan.

"We think that Ashton might have been targeted."

Derek cleared his throat. Jordan cast a look at the pictures on the mantel, showing Mr. Mayfield with a man her age, and two younger women. Their daughters? The conclusion sent a chill down her spine. The pattern.

Mrs. Mayfield spoke, "Because he was gay? That wouldn't surprise me. I don't advocate violence, don't get me wrong, but no, I'm not surprised at all. We tried so hard with him. He was just so stubborn."

"Is that why you didn't put up any pictures of him?"

Jordan tried not to let the anger bubbling up inside her color the tone of her voice. Mrs. Mayfield's hard look was indication she hadn't tried hard enough.

"You have no grounds to judge us, Detective. Ashton chose a life of sin over his family. It pains me to say it, but he's been dead to us for a long time."

Jordan wasn't sure what she had expected. There was no routine notification of death, no prediction as to how a family member would react. She didn't think she'd ever dealt with anything like this.

"Are you serious?"

At the same time, Derek asked, "When did you last speak to your son?"

"I have two beautiful daughters," Mrs. Mayfield said. "We last spoke to Ashton seven years ago. We gave him a choice, but he insisted on going against God and nature, so we told him to leave. He ended up living with his aunt, a half sister of mine who had rejected God as well, and now they're both dead."

"You kicked out your son not knowing if he had somewhere to go? Well, I guess that under the circumstances, he was better off anywhere but with you."

"Jordan," Derek warned, but she ignored him.

"Your son was murdered, and all you have to say, all you can do is repeat those bigoted phrases? Do you even begin to understand how badly you failed him as a parent? How abusive your behavior was?"

Mrs. Mayfield stood stiffly, arms wrapped around herself.

"I don't know your parents, but they sure didn't teach you any manners. I don't have to let you treat me like this, especially in my home. Be sure, Detective Carpenter, that I will file a complaint with your department."

"You do that." Jordan stalked out of the room, but not before she heard Derek use the words "apologies" and "particularly difficult case."

When he had caught up with her where they had parked down the block, she directed her frustration at him.

"You apologized? Really? Did you hear what she said?"

"I heard every single word. Damn it, Jordan. That didn't belong there. It was downright stupid."

She winced. Derek didn't use insults to make his point. Maybe she'd come to a point where she had stopped listening to reason.

"I don't need you to tell me that. I couldn't stand her, that blatant ignorance and self-righteousness. She's his mother, and she made it look like it was his fault he was murdered!"

"Yes, I know. I was there."

"You have no idea." This time, it took her only a split-second to realize the impact of her words. "I didn't mean it like that," she added with a sigh.

"I know you didn't. Because you've never been pulled over by a fellow officer for a bogus reason, wondering how this might turn out."

"What? That happened here?"

"It does."

"Not to me, you're right." she admitted. "I'm sorry. I shouldn't have gone off on her like that."

"You shouldn't have, but I get it."

Jordan indulged the brief hug, stepping back just in time. She didn't need this moment to get any more emotional. Knowing that she and Derek were back on the same page was enough for now. She'd likely hear from Carroll, and she'd have to pull herself together until then.

"I got your back with the lieutenant, but I need you to lay low for the rest of the day."

"I have no intention of doing anything else."

At least the worst part of this day was over.

Chapter Eight

J ordan didn't quite know what to make of the call she received from Detective Ann McCoy.

"I'm so sorry, but I won't be able to make it today. Something came up...I can't leave here right now."

"That happens. I understand." She paused, wondering if McCoy was going to share anything else with her.

"I'd still like to meet with you if that's okay."

"Of course. We'll reschedule. Just let me know when you can be here."

"Thank you so much. I'll get back to you as soon as possible," McCoy promised and ended the call. No more details, then.

Jordan was in the midst of updating the file on Mayfield when Carroll appeared in the doorway of his office.

"Carpenter, could you come in here for a second?"

"Sir. Of course." That didn't sound too bad, did it?

She had barely closed the door behind her when he thundered, "Have you lost your mind?"

She had expected a few words from him, but his anger surprised and irritated her. She knew she had overstepped, but she didn't think she deserved this kind of reprimand.

"Sir, with all due respect—"

"Nothing good ever comes after someone starts a sentence that way. I can't believe this from you. You told a mother whose son died that she was a bad parent?"

"Because she was. They kicked him out of his home for only one reason, because he was gay!"

"I see. What if she had regrets? What if she was simply repeating what others had told her to say? In any case, it's not your job to read her mind, however justified your feelings might be."

"Might be?" Jordan winced at realizing her voice had gone up a notch.

"Let me put it clearer. I assume most decent people would feel the same way you do, but it wasn't your job to educate her, and I'm afraid her husband's lawyer will agree with that assessment. I understand this is a tough case, especially after what you've been through."

"That has nothing to do with it."

"Doesn't it? Listen, take the afternoon, the rest of the week even. Spend some time with your kid."

Gritting her teeth was all she could do not to respond, even though Jordan knew she needed both.

"It will put things into perspective. Meanwhile, I'll try to contain the politics of this."

"Will I still have a job on Monday?" That might be melodramatic, but she couldn't help it. It was that kind of day.

"Like I said, take some time. I expect this to blow over, but it would help if you kept a low profile for a bit. They might ask you to apologize."

"Okay. I understand."

"Do you?"

She shook her head and spun around on her heel, barely keeping herself from slamming the door on the way out. Derek stood so close to the office she nearly ran into him.

"How did it go?"

"Did you know he was going to send me home? In the middle of this case?" She kept her voice low, given that the attention of most people in the room was on them already.

"I didn't know, but I had a suspicion. Do you need anything?"

"I'm fine." Given what he'd revealed in their earlier conversation and considering that nothing about this situation was his fault, Jordan preferred not to deepen the subject. She turned off her computer and picked up her keys and coat. "I'll talk to you later. Bye." He didn't try to stop her, but his concerned expression said enough. Jordan left the building and went to her car. She had barely driven a couple of miles when her cell phone rang. Ellie was probably worried, too, but she couldn't talk to her right now. Instead, she pulled into the parking lot of a fast-food chain and sent her a text message.

I'm okay. I'll be home with Meri.

Resisting the urge to answer her frustration with fried food, she drove home.

Pauline was having a coffee while Meri was playing on the floor. She didn't seem surprised to see Jordan.

"I guess Ellie called you. Do you two know more than I do?"

"She didn't give me many details. Is everything okay?"

Jordan cringed at the memory of what had seemed the only realistic response an hour ago. She picked up Meri, smiling at her enthusiastic greeting, though there was really nothing to be happy about. She had screwed up by letting her emotions sabotage her.

"I can't talk about it. But I can take over now. I'll have the rest of the week off."

"I made coffee. Let's sit for a bit."

It was the last thing Jordan wanted, but she couldn't kick out Pauline who had helped them so much. It was unthinkable that she or Jack could have ever reacted the way the Mayfields had.

Kathryn certainly had no talking room when it came to judging anyone's life, but Jordan had never heard her mention her sexual orientation once.

Maybe Jordan was the one who didn't understand. And no decent person would understand or justify words and actions such as the Mayfields'.

Then again, it wasn't like she hadn't dealt with less than decent people before on this job.

"I could go for a coffee," she said.

"You two sit, I'll get it." Pauline reached out to tousle Meri's hair. "What a nice surprise that Mommy is here, isn't it?" Meri smiled brightly.

Jordan hoped that Pauline would be gone by the time Ellie returned, just so that she could have a moment to herself, come up with a plausible explanation, something other than she hadn't pulled herself together as well as she'd thought.

Ellie could read well enough between the lines of Jordan's text message: She was okay for the moment, but not in the mood to talk. Ellie couldn't afford to dwell: She needed to focus on her work. In the briefing room, she added Ashton Mayfield's photo to the board.

Mayfield's parents hadn't reported him missing. They knew he had been living with his aunt but never contacted him. Ellie wholeheartedly agreed with Jordan's assessment of their parenting style and skills, and she also agreed with everyone who thought that it would have been wiser to keep it to herself. Scolding them didn't bring the young man back. It didn't solve the puzzle as to who had killed him.

But at some point, it had to stop. Someone had to step up and point out the harm being done.

She had tried to listen closely, and she didn't think Jordan was in danger of losing her job, but there was money in bigotry.

Ellie was still feeling conflicted when she went home that night, but she bought dinner on the way. The conversation they were going to have might not be short or easy. She'd do what she could to add a little comfort at least.

Jordan met her in the hallway.

"Hey," she said. "I'm glad you're home."

After Ellie had set the bags of food on a chair, Jordan walked straight into her embrace.

"Me too." Ellie held on tightly, before she stepped back. "How about dinner, bedtime for Meri, and then I'll ask you about your day?"

"I could live without the last part, but yes. Sounds like a plan. I'm really sorry."

"I know."

"As frustrated as I was with getting scolded, Carroll was right. It's good to be with Meri."

"I can imagine. I got Thai."

That brought a smile to Jordan's face. "You're the best wife ever."

"Don't I know it."

Ellie was more than happy to leave the conversation in a lighter place until Meri was asleep. It wasn't that long ago that she'd let her own emotions get in the way, confronted with the woman who had nearly taken everything from her...but that was different, wasn't it? Jordan was different. Ellie had always admired her ability to detach herself when a job needed to be done, to keep the bigger picture in mind.

But here they were. A grumpy Lieutenant Carroll had fielded calls from the Mayfields, their lawyer, and a couple of reporters. This was potentially serious beyond the private scope.

She tried to keep those thoughts at bay while they were having dinner and getting Meri ready for bed. Jordan didn't volunteer any more information either, sticking to the plan.

Eventually, they sat down in the living room with another glass of wine.

"I know you're worried," Jordan sat. "I'm sorry. I went too far. People have told me already, and I see their point. Whatever someone tells them or not, their son was murdered because of the killer's bigoted views, and they'll have to live with that."

"I think everyone understands. But Carroll will need some reassurances."

"Like an apology? Whatever. Hell, I'll do it. Like I said, they will have to live with themselves."

"Like knowing it won't happen again. That you're okay."

"I am. End of story. Let's not go down that road again."

"Jordan, please."

Jordan's expression showed alarm, but to Ellie's relief, she didn't leave the room. They had come to a place where they were much better than that at communicating. That didn't mean it was easy for either of them.

"What do you want me to say? Every case can be a reminder of something, honestly, no one cares. It's just that woman...I'm sure she was influenced by her husband, and her family before that, but this was her son! How dare they?" Jordan took a deep breath. "Regardless, I know it wasn't my place, not in that context. Carroll had to react—I respect that. I'll take a step back, and I'll go back to work next week."

"Are you sure that will be enough?"

There was an air of resignation in Jordan's tone when she said, "If it's not, we will find out Monday morning, right?"

"You know, I meant what I said. If you need to make some changes, we can work with that. You've mentioned you had...doubts about the job, even before today."

"Unless Carroll tells me otherwise, I'll be back on Monday. I promise I'll tell you if anything changes."

Ellie knew Jordan wasn't making that promise lightly. "I'm counting on it."

"You can trust me. I'm not going to do anything stupid like that, ever again. Our family is more important to me than banging my head against a wall. Thank you for being so patient. I know it's early, but would you mind if we went to bed?"

Ellie had imagined addressing a couple of other subjects, like the status of the case, or the fact that the detective from out of town hadn't arrived yet. She assumed those could wait a few hours.

Later when they were in bed, her arms wrapped around Jordan, she admitted to herself that she was well aware they'd only tackled the surface. She appreciated a moment of calm, before whatever storm would be next.

They would make it through as always.

Chapter Nine

I t didn't look like anyone was calling for Jordan to be fired. Ellie was grateful for a fairly quiet morning after leaving her wife and daughter at home. When the phone on Jordan's desk rang, she jumped to her feet to answer it.

"This is Detective Harding, how can I help you?"

"Oh, hi." The woman sounded surprised. "Could I speak to Detective Carpenter, please? Detective McCoy."

"She's not here today, but perhaps I can help you?"

"If you could tell her I'm sorry, and I'll definitely be there tomorrow?"

"I'll pass it on," Ellie said. She didn't think she needed to reveal that Jordan wouldn't be in this week. Whatever Detective McCoy had to contribute, she could discuss it with her and Derek. "I hope everything's okay?"

"Well, I wouldn't go that far," the detective said dryly. "I could carve out some time, and I think it will be better if we talk in person."

"Yes, I agree. We don't have any news on Tim Caplan, but we have another body. Could be a copycat. We can't say for sure yet."

"Damn." In one single word, McCoy summed up how everyone was feeling about this development.

"Yeah. We'll update you once you arrive."

"Thank you, I appreciate it. I'll see you tomorrow."

"Yes, you will," Ellie said out loud after she'd ended the call.

"What was that about?" Derek asked as he sat a coffee and donut on her desk. Some things were still blissfully predictable.

"The detective who's coming to see Jordan...I guess she'll have to make do with the two of us."

"Well, she'll be fine. We're pretty cool too. Hold that thought," Derek said when his own phone rang. Seeing the surprise in his expression only seconds after he'd answered, Ellie hoped it wasn't bad news. He seemed puzzled.

"That's interesting. Yes, I'll get the ball rolling. Thank you." His call, too, was short. "I'll be damned. I'm afraid you won't have time for a snack. Let's get a couple of uniforms."

"And go where?"

"Mr. Cordell's. He consented to a DNA test and guess what happened."

Ellie was on her feet in an instant. "No way."

"Way. It's a match. It was his blood on the branch."

"Finally, something makes sense in this."

If they were lucky, Cordell would open up about his motives and maybe help unravel the horror story surrounding Salter and whoever had decided to follow his pattern.

Cordell wasn't just surprised to be arrested, he was outraged.

"I told you I didn't do anything. If you believe otherwise, you're doing a sloppy job."

Ellie suppressed a wince. He was either a brilliant actor or—what? DNA didn't lie. No one had done a sloppy job.

"I know my rights," he said angrily. "I won't say anything to you until my lawyer is here."

"Of course. You can call them at the station."

Derek shrugged once he was in the back of the squad car. "You might still have time for your donut. It doesn't look like he'll be talking anytime soon."

"It's strange. He doesn't seem delusional to me, but he's acting like he's convinced the test was supposed to exonerate him."

"He claimed those bruises came from medication," Derek recalled.

"It could be possible. And given the amount of blood at the scene, his hands should be shredded, not just scratched," Ellie said, making him wince.

"You have a point, but I've seen stranger things. We'll figure out the bigger picture. How's Jordan doing?"

Ellie wished she didn't hesitate when confronted with that question. "Better," she said eventually. "I kind of understand why she said it, though I know it wasn't the best thing to do."

"I guess we all feel that way. I haven't seen her lose her cool like this, not on the job. I have to admit I'm worried."

"We're dealing with it. Now, you and I have a job to do." Ellie found it necessary to draw a line. She couldn't be in two places at once. Jordan was safe at home with Meri, for the time being. Everything else, they'd have to deal with later, and she didn't need a reminder that they still had some issues to address.

"Yeah, whenever that lawyer gets here."

※

"Detective Harding, it's so good to see you!"

Ellie got to her feet to shake James McKenzie's hand. This was a pleasant surprise. She knew she could work with McKenzie who was a friend of Jordan's, and by proxy, now an acquaintance of hers. They crossed paths on the job and, every once in a while, at the *D&T*.

"Same here. You're the legal representation for Mr. Cordell."

"Yes. I'm pretty sure we can work this out quickly. I had some research done after my conversation with Mr. Cordell, and he wants to talk to you."

"That's good to hear. Let's do it."

"You'll also find that he's innocent."

Ellie caught Derek's skeptical look.

"You are aware that we found your client's blood on the murder weapon, along with the victim's?"

"Let's start at the beginning," McKenzie suggested. "This will all be clear in a matter of minutes, I can assure you."

They went into the room where Cordell was already waiting, and McKenzie greeted his client.

Ellie sat across from the suspect.

"Mr. Cordell, Mr. McKenzie tells us you want to talk."

"That's right. I want to repeat to you, I didn't do anything. I knew Salter a little, didn't like him. That's as close as I ever got to him. You can ask the people in my building. I spend most of the time home. Nothing changed. I don't have transportation anyway."

"You mentioned that you didn't drive. There's still the matter of the blood on the branch Mr. Salter was beaten with. Yours."

Cordell shook his head. "See, that's impossible."

"Well, there are possibilities," McKenzie added. "One would be that my client is the suspect you're looking for, but that's already extremely unlikely based on what we know. You will find that the bruises and scratches you see are side effects of his medication. Skin breaks easier. Another possibility is that at one point, one of those blood samples was mishandled."

"Come on, James, that's a low blow," Ellie said. "We double-checked with the lab. The sample that was taken at the department matches the one taken from the branch. Mr. Cordell's."

"Oh, I didn't say it was someone at the department who made the mistake. Doesn't all of this sound too easy for you?"

"Sometimes it is that easy," Derek answered.

"You were a coach for most of your professional life," Ellie addressed Cordell. "You knew Salter, maybe noticed that he was preying on young men, maybe teenagers, even. Wanting to stop him, that's understandable."

"No, you got this wrong," Cordell protested. "I knew about the wife and the son, yes, but I didn't know the exact nature of the abuse. If I had been privy to anything that happened on my watch, I would have called the police. I swear! I haven't thought about him in years, to be honest. I spent the past few years in pain, with doctors trying to figure out what to do."

"You're aware that Mr. Cordell took part in a clinical trial a few years ago. That required many blood samples between then and now. I have faith that the people in your lab did everything by the book, but what if the blood came from another lab?"

"To frame Mr. Cordell?"

"Is that so far-fetched? The person would be aware that you wouldn't need long to connect the dots. You'd identify the medication in the blood sample, realize it was a fairly rare substance, and trace it down to Mr. Cordell. Who actually knew Mr. Salter. It all fits perfectly."

Unfortunately, Ellie had to admit he had a point. If that was the case, they'd walked right into the trap. She cast a glance at Cordell, noticing the thin sheen of sweat on his forehead. Was he in pain—or hiding something? Both?

"It does, doesn't it? But it would be equally hard to prove that someone involved with the drug trial dropped the ball."

Ellie knew his response before he said, "True, but enough for reasonable doubt? This is not a case the D.A. will want to take to court."

"Well, we'll see about that." She looked at Mr. Cordell again. He was clearly uncomfortable. She was taking a shot in the dark. "Let's be reasonable. If you want me to believe you, Mr. Cordell, I need you to tell me the whole truth, anything that could help us."

"I didn't kill anyone."

"But you knew something?"

She knew she was going in the right direction when he looked away. Ellie waited. McKenzie looked resigned. It took almost a minute before Cordell spoke,

"I thought about it a lot lately. Back in the day, we didn't know everything we know now."

She suppressed a sigh, fairly sure that they'd hear the type of explanation that people brought up when they tried to avoid being held accountable. Different times?

"What exactly does that mean?"

"There was a boy, at the time, I think he had a summer job at the place where Salter was the foreman. He was also...a homosexual. Not that there's anything wrong with it," he added quickly, "but the guys on the team gave him a hard time."

"You didn't do anything about it."

Cordell had the good grace to look ashamed. "I thought they were figuring it out among themselves, but now...Look, there was no gay marriage at the time or anything. It wasn't a 'thing' like now."

"What happened?"

Ellie was fairly proud of herself for keeping her tone neutral. Jordan might have gone a few steps too far. Ellie could feel the temptation to roll her eyes, at least. This was no laughing matter.

"One day, he didn't come to training, and the next thing I heard was that he'd run away. Thinking back...I wish I'd said something."

"That would have been the appropriate thing to do, as you were in a position of power."

"Regardless," McKenzie said, "Mr. Cordell might have done something questionable in the past, but that doesn't make him a murderer. In fact, what you have here is probably another piece of the puzzle in Salter's case."

"I agree. But he didn't kill himself."

"If he murdered all those boys, why does anyone care?" Cordell wondered out loud.

Ellie didn't say it out loud, but part of her would have agreed with him, if it wasn't for the recent murder. "I'd like to speak to Mr. McKenzie for a moment."

"Sure."

McKenzie was on his feet in an instant while Derek stayed with Mr. Cordell.

"Could I get you a coffee?" Ellie heard him ask.

Outside the room, she and McKenzie walked a few steps.

"I'm not making any promises," she said. "We'll look into the pharmaceutical company. Unless we can find definitive evidence that someone could have stolen blood samples, I'm afraid the A.D.A. will want to go forward."

"We'll cross that bridge if we get to it. Is there anything else you wanted to talk about?"

There was no scorn in his voice, just genuine interest.

"Not really. I just had to warn you."

"I appreciate it. And yes, I'm as disgusted as you are, but at least he realizes he was wrong. I believe in choosing your battles, and at the moment, that's trying to make you see that my client is not a murderer."

"The A.D.A. might be open to a deal, considering who the victim was. So you heard." Ellie hadn't meant to say the last part out loud, but now she couldn't take it back.

"Yeah, I did. Is Jordan okay?"

"She will be."

"That's good. Tell her I said hi, and don't let them take anything, especially not the job that puts a roof over your head."

"I'll tell her you said that."

"Thanks. Now, about bail for Mr. Cordell?"

"A judge will decide that," she said.

"You were really good in there, Detective. This was clearly something he'd been carrying with him for a long time."

Chapter Ten

E llie returned home late once again, the various aspects of the case and the conversations she'd had, still vivid on her mind. Jordan greeted her at the door, looking a lot less exhausted than she had two days ago.

If this break helped her, Ellie was all for it. She was also feeling guilty for immersing herself in her work in the past few hours and fairly enjoying it. Not the content, of course. The fact that Derek had let her do most of the interrogation, and McKenzie's praise, hadn't gone unnoticed with her.

But she couldn't tell Jordan how to feel about the job.

"Hey. You two had a good day?"

"Perfect. Kathryn came by, so I even had the time to take a nap. I'm sorry, Meri's already asleep."

"I figured. It's okay. I'll just sneak in for a moment, and then we can eat?"

When she returned from Meri's room, Ellie noticed that Jordan had cooked chicken and rice and prepared a salad. She had set the table in the kitchen.

"This looks great. I'm starving."

"I imagine. I talked to Derek earlier, and he told me you moved forward with Cordell. That, and you did a pretty good job getting him to talk."

"It wasn't that hard. He might still make bail."

"Yeah, James can be a pain, but he has good instincts. If he says something is worth considering, it probably is."

"I agree. To everything you said." Ellie laughed, though she recalled what he'd said about choosing battles. What if you weren't sure what the right ones were? What if you'd fought so many battles that you needed a break?

"Anyway, Detective McCoy will join us tomorrow. We'll give her an update on the case."

"Good." Jordan's expression turned serious. She grew quiet, as if searching for the right words.

"It will be okay," Ellie felt the need to say something. "We'll update her on what we have."

"Sure...Ellie. I wasn't lying. The past couple of days have been good, but at the same time, not working is freaking me out."

"I know. It always does."

"It's different. I never doubted that I could still do the job, but I think the lieutenant does right now."

"Forget about the lieutenant for a moment. I know his opinion matters, but he understands the context. Besides, he hasn't said anything. He told you to take the week. I still believe that's all. I need to know what *you* want."

Jordan shrugged. "I want to go back to a time before it happened, but I can't. I wish I knew. All I know is that much of the past year has been all about me, and I'm tired of it. I'm...ashamed." Her calm tone struck Ellie, testimony to how much time she'd spent defining that emotion.

"Seriously, why? You've worked so hard to get here, of course it's tiring. You made a mistake, but I have news for you. I've made them. Everyone has. That's not a reason to be ashamed."

"I know I'm not the only one who had crappy things happen to them. You didn't risk your job. I didn't see Sam doing it either."

Ellie was beginning to have a clearer picture as to where their conversation was headed.

"Still no reason, believe me. Maybe I did rush things in the past. It's not a competition, that's what you said to Sam, right? I believe you said the same thing to me once. Do you know how freaking proud I am of you, of us?"

Jordan looked startled, but maybe it was because Ellie's eyes were welling up.

"It's true, we've had some 'crappy things' happen to us. We did our best to deal with them, and we didn't blame anyone else. Can't say the same thing for Danny Roth or Joy Anne Deane."

"Please don't cry," Jordan said, reaching out to take her hands. "I see your point. I swear I do. Perhaps I needed a reminder."

"That's what I'm here for," Ellie confirmed, her voice still a tad shaky. "I love you, and I love Meri. Everything else, we'll figure out."

Jordan pulled her close, growling stomachs reminding them that they hadn't had dinner yet.

<hr/>

Even though the evening had ended on a light note, Jordan was aware that she had some uncomfortable conversations ahead. With her boss, to reassure him he could still count on her. With her partner, for similar reasons. But everything was clear and talked out with Ellie, which was the most important thing.

Jordan didn't want to do quit her job, even if lately, it felt like the cost was higher than the reward. Partly, that was the nature of things. She'd have to do a better job at self-care.

Jordan had felt raw and vulnerable for a long time now. The Mayfields' bigotry had been a trigger, though unrelated to her own experiences. Her biological mother and her husband were addicts. They'd been negligent, but they weren't homophobic. Clearly, she wasn't the right person to show Mrs. Mayfield and her husband the light—and if that had been her intention, she hadn't done a good job at it.

Ellie was already in bed when she returned from the bathroom, probably ready to go to sleep. Slipping under the covers, Jordan leaned into the warmth of her body with a sigh of relief.

"Thank you," she whispered, placing a kiss on her neck, a way to say goodnight maybe, but then the need to touch became almost overwhelming, her hands starting to wander under the covers.

"I see you have some ideas on how to express your gratitude," Ellie whispered back, smiling.

It had been hard to admit, to herself in the first place, that she still needed time to heal. It was taking longer with every close call.

Ellie was right, they had so much. So much to hold on to, to be proud of. She'd be back at work next Monday.

Moments later, the sheets and their nightwear were on the floor.

Ellie's hands on her body did their usual magic.

Jordan held her breath when fingertips brushed over a scar but didn't linger. The feeling of being trapped vanished in the rush of pleasure.

The next day, Ellie made it to the station with only a few minutes to spare. She didn't mind the rushed morning. She was well aware that they'd had a breakthrough, touched on some important subjects. Their shared intimacy always had the power to bring them back on track. She had intended to get herself a coffee quickly, nearly running into someone familiar-looking in the break room.

"Oh...You're back."

"Hi! Detective Harding, right?" Izzy said. "It seems like your fridge is in more trouble."

"Please, don't say it out loud," Maria Doss joked. "I'm not sure the boss will find money in the budget for a new one." Her amused gaze told Ellie that she, too, had caught on the fact that the young repairwoman was flirting with her.

"I just wanted a coffee," she said.

"I was going to take a break. If you have time, you could maybe join me?"

"I'm sorry, but I'm going to need Detective Harding," Doss rescued her. "Another time."

When they were outside, Ellie told her, "Thank you so much. I mean, it's flattering, but it's a bit much. Unless...You actually needed me for something?"

"Not at this moment, no."

"Good. Derek and I will be in court for Cordell's bail hearing. Would you mind keeping an eye out for any messages that come in during that time?"

"Of course. Should I take any messages from Izzy?"

"Funny. Please, don't."

❦

The hearing went as expected, with Cordell making bail at a sum high enough to fit the charges. He had cooperated, and McKenzie made the point that Cordell didn't present a flight risk.

"I didn't expect anything else after yesterday," A.D.A. Esposito admitted when they left the building together. "Get to that pharmaceutical lab soon so we can rule them out."

"I hope it will show that you can drop the charges against my client," McKenzie, who had caught up with them, said. "In any case, I'll be more than happy to share information. I'm sure there's a lot to learn."

"I'll see you later," was Valerie's response. Ellie saw that Derek had already gone to the car.

"I haven't seen you at the *SEVEN* in a while, though I've talked to your parents-in-law," McKenzie said. "You think you and Jordan might be around tonight?"

"I'm not sure. Perhaps I shouldn't be seen with you in public until this case is closed, and she is still on leave."

"Sure, but she can have a drink, right?"

"I'll ask her if she's up for it. Before I forget, she said to tell you you're a pain."

He burst into laughter. "That sounds like Carpenter."

"And that your instincts are usually right on the money. I'll let you know if I find anything about the company."

"Same here. Thank you."

Chapter Eleven

E llie had sat down behind her desk when Officer Marshall arrived with a woman in her late thirties wearing a visitor's badge. She got to her feet before Libby could introduce her.

"Detective McCoy, it's nice to meet you. I'm Detective Harding. I'll bring you up to speed today."

"Thank you, I appreciate it. I'm sorry for messing with your schedule these last couple of days. I couldn't leave without taking care of a few things first."

"Don't worry about it." Ellie could have told her that they had some experience with unexpected incidents messing up the schedule, but she kept those thoughts to herself. "Your timing is actually perfect. Our suspect in the Charles Salter murder made bail and is awaiting trial, and we can focus all our resources on the victims. I'll show you where to get coffee first...Believe me, that's going to be of importance."

"I don't doubt it." The other woman smiled. "And please, call me Ann. Since I'm going to be here a while."

"Thanks. I'm Ellie."

They walked to the break room where they got coffee. Ann McCoy bought a chocolate bar from the vending machine.

"For later," she said with a hint of apology. "By the way, when do you think I could meet Detective Carpenter?"

"Something came up, but this an all hands on deck situation. Detective Henderson and I will provide you with everything you need."

Ann gave her a nod in answer, her attention drawn to the board the moment they walked into the briefing room. She stepped closer, taking in every detail, the photographs, the information, the arrows connecting names and stories. Charles Salter. Eric Salter. The human remains found in the Salters' basement, some still unidentified. Missing persons that fit Salter's victims' profile. Ashton Mayfield. Recent missing persons. Question marks.

She stopped in front of Tim Caplan's photo.

"As you know he was seen by a trucker who let him off at a rest stop close by," Ellie commented. "He bought a coffee and left. We lost his trail after that."

"His parents..." Ann shook her head. "Their son ran away because they wanted to send him to some 'gay conversion camp,'—yet they have nothing better to do than make accusations."

"Like what?"

"Baseless. They think his professor made him gay because she is."

That sounded suspiciously like Ashton Mayfield's parents. Jordan might have chosen a questionable context, but what she'd told them was nothing but the truth.

"I'm sorry, and also, what is wrong with these people?" Ellie didn't think she'd have to tiptoe around the detective.

"Excellent question."

"Actually, it was a rhetorical one. So, this is something most of the victims have in common: They were estranged from their parents at a young age for similar reasons. Salter preyed on young men, and teenagers. According to the son he had an interest in college sports. Some of his victims were athletes in local teams, others co-workers in the factory where he was the foreman. It's circumstantial, of course, but the most plausible explanation. Now we have a new victim that fits the profile to a T, but by the time he was murdered, Salter was already dead."

"A copycat?"

"That's what we assume. So far, we've kept certain details out of the press. It's definitely someone who has familiarized themselves with the case."

"Any doubts that Salter is the original killer?"

Ellie was glad they got coffee. This was going to be a long day.

"Not really. The bones were in the house that he owned and lived in for decades. He took vacations near your jurisdiction. If someone tried to frame him, it would be one huge conspiracy. Everyone who knew him said he was a wife beater and a homophobe who didn't hold back his opinions. Lots of anger...and self-loathing, I assume, but about that part, we might never know."

"And the copycat dumped a body in the backyard of the woman who found Salter. That's a twisted sense of humor," McCoy said wryly.

"You could say that. We're still waiting on tests from the scene. Everything is backed up since we found out Salter wasn't just a victim."

"I can imagine. What about the son, Eric Salter?"

"We looked at him closely. Not much love lost between him and his father, and yes, we thought he was a little eager to provide means and opportunity for Charles...but other than that, nothing. He has an alibi, works out of town."

"Hm. Okay."

Ellie waited. From Jordan, she usually could interpret a monosyllabic response. She wasn't so sure now.

"We're trying to tie together these cases and see where there could have been potential witnesses. The factory is one of those places, but as you can see, the cases span over years." She followed Ann's gaze, the names, too many of them, grouped into the different categories. If they could tie a victim to a missing persons case, the year they disappeared was marked next to the name.

Too many question marks.

"Excuse me for a second?"

"Of course."

Ellie wasn't sure if the thought that sprang to her mind was helpful, or just an obvious detail of the horrific story that had been unfolding over the past week. At her desk, she jotted down a few notes for information to check, suppressing a sigh when she realized she still had calls to make. She'd promised Valerie Esposito that her case wouldn't fall apart like McKenzie had suggested.

This was priority.

Jordan picked up on the second ring.

"Hey," she said, surprised. "Everything okay?"

"With me, yes. I need to ask you something. Maybe I'm completely off, but this could be important."

"Now I'm intrigued."

"Okay, Granger and Hunt. I'm looking at the timeline here...So far, in every case that fits the pattern, the victims had little or no contact with their families. I was wondering, in some of those cases, do we know the actual moment they went missing?"

"Go on." Jordan had snapped into professional mode with ease. Ellie took a moment to acknowledge how relieved she felt about that fact.

"And Ashton Mayfield? What happened after his aunt died? He had a number of jobs, and eventually, we lose the trace. Perhaps he stayed with a friend, or he couldn't get a credit card, but I think there's another explanation..."

"That son of a bitch," Jordan said, understanding what Ellie was saying. "He kept them."

For a few seconds, they were both silent, wrestling with the possibilities.

"I'll talk to Dr. Adams again, see if there's anything to support that theory. The Grangers and the Hunts hadn't heard from their sons in years, and even Hunt's sister, who was somewhat supportive, didn't know about his whereabouts in the past eighteen months."

"Good call. I think that's important with regard to the Mayfield case."

Jordan sounded pensive.

"I hate what this likely means, but I'm glad you see it too. I have Ann—Detective McCoy—here. I'll get Derek and bring this to the lieutenant."

"You do that. You're on a first name basis already?" Jordan asked, amused. "What's she like?"

"Okay, so far. And she offered. Everything good at home?" She appreciated Jordan's attempt of lighting up the conversation, but there wasn't much time, and she needed to know.

"Perfect. We just settled on the couch for some cartoons."

With mixed emotions, Ellie listened to the sounds of Meri playing in the background. She would have loved to be there. At the same time, she wished that Jordan was back at work so they could bounce off ideas in person.

"Sounds good. I'm sorry, I really have to get back to work. Thanks for listening."

"Any time."

After ending the call, Ellie picked up her notes and went to return to their guest, meeting Derek on the way.

"You're here, good. I have something to tell you."

"Same here," he said.

Every once in a while, he dreamed about the book he was going to write, the interviews he was going to give once he'd made it out of this place.

How did you survive hell?

The food wasn't so bad. Three meals a day for the captive. Captives? It had been quiet for a while, no one answering from the other room. Ashton was gone.

He hadn't seen or heard anything, but this couldn't be good. Which was a ridiculous thing to think, because nothing about this was any good.

There were times when he thought about trying to formulate a plan. About reasoning with the man. There were times when he thought his parents had been right, and if only he'd listened to them, he wouldn't be in this situation.

There were times when he wondered if he was losing his mind. He was going to die, maybe sometime soon, maybe a long time from now. Or, if he managed to convince the man during one of his friendlier phases...

He heard the creaking of a door nearby, the same door falling shut and being locked. A moment later, a voice called out, "Help! Anybody? I need help!"

It wasn't good, for his temporary companion who sounded just as angry, desperate and scared. He couldn't help feeling relieved at the sound of a human voice.

"Hey. I'm afraid I can't help you." He inched closer to the wall, as close as the chains allowed. "But we can talk. What's you name? I'm Tim."

Ellie's theory made sense. It was haunting Jordan, the idea of a kidnapper who prepared to keep his victims for a long time before he killed them. She didn't need much of an imagination to envision what happened between the abduction and the murder. It was like a combination of worst-case scenarios wrapped together. She hated that it brought her back to some of the worst moments of her life. The images were vivid even as she sat in a sun-filled room with her daughter in her arms.

Ellie had sounded stressed, too. Everyone had a lot on their plate with these multiplying cases. Jordan was aware that she hadn't made it easier on her co-workers and friends.

"I'm really sorry," she whispered to Meri, before she picked up her phone and called Pauline. To her relief, the conversation was quick and easy. The next call wouldn't be.

"I know it's probably a bad time, but would you have a moment?"

"This is a surprise."

"I'd like to talk in person if that's possible. And...I'd like to come back to work. Today."

She'd almost said, need, and that was as close to the truth. Being home with Meri had helped her clear her mind like nothing else. She couldn't hide from the world any longer when she needed to do her share.

Chapter Twelve

J ordan was lucky. Lieutenant Carroll agreed to see her, and she made it into his office unseen, another testimony as to how busy everyone was.

"Thank you for seeing me," she said, still in her coat. More than anything, she wanted to get this over with.

"I don't have much time, but I get the feeling this is important. How are you doing?"

She wished people wouldn't feel the need to ask her that all the time.

"Good, thank you. I hear there's a lot going on."

"Look, I have nothing against you coming back to work, but if I put you back on that case, I need you to be able to handle it. Unfit parents and all, they are not the suspects here."

"I understand what I did was unprofessional."

"It sure was."

"You won't have to worry about it. I'm sorry for the trouble I caused the department."

"I know," he said with a sigh. "This is taking a toll on everyone, but I need you all to keep it together. Go find Harding and Henderson and get to work."

"Thank you, sir."

"The Mayfields still want an apology," he said. "They have given you until Monday night, but since you're here, might as well get that over with too."

She straightened. "I'll take care of it."

⁂

Ellie was alone in the break room, frowning over a pile of files.

"Hello there," Jordan said, softly closing the door behind her.

Ellie's expression was part surprise and alarm.

"Sorry. Meri's fine, I asked Pauline to stay with her. I thought about what you said. I can't be hiding at home while there's so much work to do...and I talked to Carroll."

"Oh. What did he say?"

"As long as I apologize to the Mayfields and keep it professional, I'm back."

Ellie's smile conveyed her relief. "That's so great! For many reasons, but one of them is that we're really swamped. I mean...Not that you have to apologize, but I sort of understand the politics of this. We don't have to like it."

"No...but he does have a point. I messed up, and that could have backfired in a much worse way. I'm sorry."

"We'll be okay."

Given the fact that they were still alone, Jordan walked into her embrace. "I got so angry, but that did nothing for the victims. And we will be more than okay."

They kissed, stepping apart a second too late when the door opened, and Derek walked in with another woman.

"Okay, we can get right back to it," Ellie said without a trace of self-consciousness. "Jordan, meet Detective McCoy."

It was not the introduction Jordan had imagined, but to her relief, everyone shared the same focus.

"On the bright side, the case against Cordell is holding up," Ellie explained after they'd sat around the table in the briefing room. "The clinic where he had his trial didn't notice anything about samples missing. I'm not sure how much reasonable doubt McKenzie will be able to create with this theory. So far, we haven't found anything to back it up. Now, back to the matter at hand..."

The closer they looked, the more her daunting hypothesis seemed to make sense. Hunt, Granger and Mayfield had gone missing, but their paper trail was lost, in each case, long before the official report was filed.

"I'm reluctant to put Ashton Mayfield in that category, and Tim Caplan for that matter. If the copycat continues the pattern, he must have been aware of Salter's murders for some time. Tim's story is similar to the others, but he hasn't been missing that long. If the same perp took him..."

Ann's expression was impassive, but Ellie had noticed her tense posture. Tim Caplan could be hiding from his parents. He could be the captive of a predator. "Then we might still have a chance. This is where we should focus."

No one disagreed with her.

"There's a sad story with each of them, of parents and peers failing them. Now that you've seen what we're dealing with here..." Jordan directed her question at Ann. "Is there anything you think stands out?"

"I wish I could come up with anything. He was isolated, like the others. His parents gave generous donations to the university."

"He confided in his professor," Ellie recalled.

"Yes, but I will vouch for her. She's my sister. And she told us everything they talked about."

"Did anyone else know about their conversations? I'm wondering..." Jordan let her words trail off. "Hunt had a sister, but they eventually stopped talking. Tim ran away. What if the killers didn't just prey on someone vulnerable, but they took steps to isolate them even more? Salter, and whoever continued after him, they were too damn patient. #2 might have had the chance to observe Salter, if he follows the MO so closely."

"This is getting worse by the minute," Derek observed. "He stalks them for long enough to make sure they have little to no support, finds a way to sever the last ties and then he pounces. The killing takes place months to years after? Jesus Christ."

"It all fits," Ellie concluded. "This is why we had trouble establishing a timeline. I agree, it must be someone close to Salter, not that he was close with a lot of people."

"He must have access to drugs," Ann McCoy said. "They might have been vulnerable psychologically, but they were younger, probably fitter than the kidnapper. Either they trusted him—and at least, Salter doesn't sound like that type of guy—or he found a way to overpower them."

"Oliver Boyd was seen with an older man. I don't think it was Salter senior—someone at the *D&T* would have remembered him. But the new killer? It could have been him."

"Except Boyd still doesn't fit the victim profile." Derek sounded impatient.

"Why not? He thought he might be losing his best friend after revealing he was attracted to him."

"Yeah, that's not the same. Boyd meeting that older man, and the suicide, happened in one night."

"We don't know that because we never looked. The killer might have contacted Boyd before."

"I don't think that's what Ellie suggested we should focus on. There's nothing we can do for Boyd, but Caplan might still be alive."

"Okay. Fair enough."

Jordan crossed out something on her notepad. Ellie thought she looked pale. This was a nightmare getting worse by the minute, the picture coming together as to what the victims had gone through—and the memories it evoked.

"Strong painkillers or anesthetics." Jordan tossed her pen back onto the table. "Like the medication Cordell took, and the person who killed Salter. Why do I feel like we are going around in circles?"

❦

The feeling didn't vanish, no matter how many details they put on the table. To her surprise, it was career criminal turned informant Chucky Mulveney who called her.

"You know I could be mistaken, but I thought I should tell you anyway."

"Spit it out, Chucky. I'm about to go for dinner."

"You might want to swing by Rigley's first." Mulveney had taken over the bar from its previous owner and had been leading a law-abiding life since his last arrest. "That kid you're looking for, I think I saw him."

Jordan suppressed the impulse to sigh. "Tim Caplan? Are you sure? When did you see him, and why are you telling me only now?"

"You're never grateful," he accused.

"What? You want a prize?"

"I wouldn't mind a reward if there is one—"

"Chucky! Focus."

"All right, all right. I saw him on the news. I didn't realize he was missing until now, so that's why I'm telling you. It was a couple of weeks ago maybe."

"Maybe?"

"Could be three, come on, you know I have a job. Good-looking boy, and I thought the guy he was with was a little too old for him."

"Instead of me going over there, I'd like you to come here. I'm going to need a description of that guy, and names of people who might have seen him."

"Whoa, Detective, slow down. The place was packed. I remember it now because there was a game on...They didn't seem to care. I thought it was odd. We were short-staffed, so I waited on a few tables including theirs."

"That's all good. I still need you to come here, now."

As Jordan checked her watch, she realized what time it was and that there was something else she'd promised to get done today.

"On second thought, ask for Harding and Henderson. They'll take your statement, you'll do the facial composite, and then we can all call it a night."

"You'll be where?"

"Sorry, Chucky. None of your business."

<hr />

It wasn't the note she wanted to end this day on, but the sooner this was over, the better. Jordan had worried they might gloat in her face. She could tell from the haggard faces of Mayfield's parents that the realization had sunk in—their son was gone forever, and no late understanding or regrets could change that fact.

"What do you want?" Mayfield asked, his wife behind him. Unlike the last time, she looked anxious. Jordan could hear voices from the living room and had a hard time not to cringe. Ashton's sisters and their families.

"I won't bother you for long. I wanted to tell you that we're doing everything we can to find Ashton's murderer, and...I'm sorry about what I said, Mrs. Mayfield. I was out of line."

"Yes, you were," he muttered. Mrs. Mayfield shrugged. "You're not doing so much if you haven't found him yet. Come back when you do."

"We'll be in touch."

He turned and walked away while his wife remained in the same spot. Jordan thought she might want to tell her something she didn't want to share in front of her husband. However, her next words were somewhat predictable.

"I know you're worried we might sue, but you're lucky we have other things on our minds, like our son's funeral."

"I'm very sorry."

"Everyone is. That doesn't change anything."

"I know. Good night, Mrs. Mayfield. If you can think of anything that might help us, please, don't hesitate to call."

"Detective Henderson left his card with us." With that, she closed the door, not quite in Jordan's face.

"Close enough," Jordan mumbled before she walked back to her car. She was surprised to realize how much lighter she felt. It didn't change that she considered the Mayfields' behavior abusive. It had bothered her that for a moment she almost didn't care whether she responded in kind.

She wanted to be better than that.

⁂

Ellie wasn't sure if Jordan would be happy with the facial composite they now had thanks to Chucky Mulveney. She didn't know how Jordan and Derek handled him—Mulveney got on her last nerve.

"Time is money, lady, detective, and I'm not making any right now. You could at least get me a coffee for my contribution?"

Derek coughed, probably covering up laughter. At least one of them had a sense of humor about the situation.

"We are grateful for your contribution, Mr. Mulveney," she said. "No need for beverages. We are done here."

"If you find him because of my tip, is there going to be a reward?"

"Mr. Caplan is missing. He's not a wanted felon."

"No rich parents offering money? That's too bad."

"Hey, Chucky. You heard what the detective said?" Derek reminded him. "Conversation's over. Come on."

"Yeah, sure, I hear you. I hope he's all right."

"Me too," Ellie said after Derek went to see him out. She cast a look at her watch, wondering if Jordan had any success with her mission. As if on cue, the subject of her thoughts walked in, looking tired but relieved.

"Hey. How did it go?"

"Okay, I guess. They said they weren't going to sue. I suppose they got a reality check."

"You think?"

Jordan shrugged. "Regarding the finality of death? I think so. The rest of it, I'm not so sure, but there's nothing I can do about it."

Ellie wished she had a better answer, but she couldn't come up with any. "At least we have the vaguest facial composite in the history of the profession which is entirely because of Mulveney. Wow, but he's annoying."

"He is," Jordan agreed with a smile."

"Could be Salter, but it's not good enough. Let's start fresh tomorrow? Jack asks if we want to come to the *SEVEN* for dinner. Pauline will bring Meri afterwards."

"Dinner sounds great," Jordan said ruefully. "I feel bad for springing babysitter duty on her."

"She's fine," Ellie reassured her. "And Meri is used to it. It was important that you came back today."

"Yes, it was."

Someone clearing their throat alerted them to the fact that they weren't alone anymore.

"I'm sorry to interrupt," Ann McCoy said. "I came here straight from my hotel, and since you mentioned dinner, I was wondering if you could recommend a place close by."

"We could," Jordan told her. "Would you like to join us?"

Chapter Thirteen

J ack was at the *SEVEN* tonight, and Jordan greeted him with a quick hug.

"I think everyone's going with the menu. Extra fries. It's been a long day."

"Sounds like it. Coming right up. For drinks?"

Everyone gave their order, and he went to the counter. Jordan got up quickly to follow him. "I wanted to say I'm sorry I made Mom come over on such short notice."

"Don't worry about it. We love being with Meri whenever possible. Everything okay?"

She nodded. "Work is a bit crazy right now. Anyway...Thank you."

"You're welcome. Relax for a bit. You can take your time with dinner."

"I don't think I can. I'm starving," she said, laughing, before she went to join her friends. Introductions had been made all around. She couldn't help wondering what Ann had made of her earlier absence and rather abrupt return to the case. If she was curious, she didn't let it show. She'd been focused and professional all day.

Derek and Kate had joined them, as well as Maria Doss and Valerie Esposito.

"I can't believe this was just one day," Esposito said. "Bail for Cordell was only this morning! We're still good, right?"

"As far as I know. Something still bothers me about those meds he was taking, and who else had access to it," Jordan admitted.

Ellie looked at her, intrigued, and she was aware of Ann following the conversation with interest, too.

"You don't think Cordell had anything to do with the other murders?"

"That's a stretch," Derek agreed with Ellie. "If he was doped up as much as that medication suggests, I don't think he had the motivation to be a serial killer."

"Mayfield fits the victim profile," Jordan mused. "Thanks to Ellie we know that Cordell had suspicions regarding Salter. He wasn't a fan, but why? Because he hated him for what he did, or because he wanted to do the same?"

"Have you talked to Dr. Roberts?" Derek and Bethany, Jordan's ex, had come to a ceasefire in the aftermath of Joy Anne Deane's attack. His question sounded mildly interested.

"Not in some time, but we might have to call in the FBI soon. We know that Tim Caplan was in town. I suppose Torres or Russo will join us if it becomes necessary. I'd prefer if we found Caplan alive."

Jack, who brought a tray with beers to their table, ended the conversation for the moment.

Jordan wasn't sure what to make of Ann's pensive gaze, but she had other things on her mind at the moment. Gratitude was one of them, though the restlessness remained. There had to be something they were still overlooking. She hoped that Mulveney's description of their suspect, vague as it was, would help move the case forward.

❧

Ellie's morning felt much like a déjà-vu, when she called the same clinic where Cordell's medication trial had taken place. This time, she spoke to a different person who was nevertheless aware of the police's inquiry.

"My colleague told me you were wondering about blood samples missing. The answer's still the same, and if you want to ask about the medication Mr. Cordell received, there was no problem either." After a small pause, Dr. Sherman added. "I normally wouldn't tell you his name, but with the warrant for our files and his arrest, I guess we're past that?"

"Thank you for the clarification, Dr. Sherman. To your knowledge, has anything else gone missing in the past few months?" She was fishing. They still assumed a connection to Cordell and the medication found in the blood on the branch, but in theory, the kidnapper/killer could have used different drugs on his victims.

Dr. Adams hadn't gotten back to her yet.

"Funny you should ask. Well, actually not funny. A nurse's aide made off with a variety of narcotics, but that was before my time. A report was filed, she was eventually arrested, but nothing much came of it. I suppose they made it onto the black market. We increased security measures afterwards, but I can assure you, no one was negligent. Employees have to pass a background check, and there's only so far you can go with that. People need to do their job."

"I understand. Was this nurse's aide, by any chance, working on the trial Mr. Cordell took part in?"

"No, that trial came later. I'm sorry I can't help you much."

"No, thank you, that's very helpful. One more thing—could you give me the name of the nurse's aide?"

"Sure. Her name was Annie Walton."

After Ellie ended the call, she ran a quick search on the case and then went back to the briefing room. "I might have something," she said.

Before she could lay out what she'd learned from the doctor, a cell phone rang. Detective McCoy picked up hers, and after a quick glance to the screen, said, "I'm sorry, I have to take this." She went to the far corner and answered.

Ellie didn't mean to overhear her words, but they weren't standing that far apart.

"That's good news," Ann said, her voice softening. "No, I'm not sure when I'll be back, but there's been some progress."

Ellie unfolded the sheets of paper she'd brought.

"I'll talk to you later," was barely audible. She remembered the previous calls and then the delay of the detective's arrival. No one's life was without complications. Ann returned to the table a moment later.

"I'm sorry," she said.

"That's fine. I might have an idea as to where the killer got the drugs to subdue his victims. A nurse's aide named Annie Walton who was caught stealing drugs."

"You think Walton sold the drugs to the killer?" Jordan asked. Ellie didn't even take a moment to worry about her skeptical tone. It meant a lot to her that Jordan was back in work mode, her focus laser sharp. That, and Ellie had an answer.

"That's what I want to ask her. She wasn't there for the trial, but we already know that someone must have started planning a long time ago. I'd like to show her the facial composite."

"It's worth a shot," Ann McCoy agreed. "When are we going?"

Ellie caught Jordan's gaze, a bit more amused than irritated. Kindred spirits. They were both used to calling the shots, but McCoy was still a guest to this investigation.

"It's fine, you two go," Jordan said. "Derek and I will check with Dr. Adams. We'll let you know if anything comes up. You'll be okay?"

It occurred to Ellie that she might prefer not to go near the prison where Joy Anne Deane served her sentence. Come to think of it, so did Natalie. It was a small world. Then she realized that Jordan might not be thinking of either one, but the fact that Ellie had been trapped in said prison during a lockdown not long ago, threatened with a gun. She could think of many places she'd rather go, but like that other time, she had a job to do. Jordan would do hers.

"I'll be fine," Ellie assured her. "We'll see you later."

"If we can trace the drugs, we might have a shot at bringing Tim home," Ellie reminded a pensive Ann when they were on the road.

"I hope we will. Anything is better than what he's going through now, right?"

"I'm afraid so. Though I hope his parents will change their minds after this." That kind of attitude felt alien to Ellie whose parents had always loved and supported her. Yet, she was aware that despite a major shift in public opinion and increased knowledge, too many kids weren't so lucky.

"I'd be surprised if they did. I guess he'll prefer that they disown him. So much unnecessary pain."

Ellie could only agree. "Let's hope this will help. He knows that your sister, at least, will stand by him."

"Her resources are somewhat limited, but yes, she will."

It had only been a couple of days, but Ellie had to suppress the impulse to ask curious questions that might be interpreted as nosy. She soon realized that Ann McCoy had some of her own.

"So, you're married...on the job, how does that work?"

"Pretty well. We don't usually go on assignments together, which, of course, makes sense...but this is different. Lives are still at stake, so that's more important than anything else."

"Of course. You worked cases like this before?"

"Once. Thank God they're not all that common."

"True. Mine aren't always murders, but lately..." Ann let her sentence trail off. "We've dealt with a few hate groups. Organized bigotry, the kind that doesn't mind the dirty work. Before I came here, I did a little research, and I realized that you were involved in the Prophets of Better Days case."

"That one kept us busy, yes."

Ellie wasn't sure if Ann was just making conversation, or if she genuinely wanted to talk about the Prophets, the cult that had started out with three megalomaniac women-hating brothers committing multiple crimes. Again, over the span of decades. They had produced a murderer and a mother who had attacked a cop rather than facing her role in losing custody for her children.

"I can imagine. They're secretive...and they'll go to great lengths for their cause. My niece was kidnapped when she was two years old. We were lucky. We got her back, and she's okay, but the people who did it never showed any remorse."

"I'm so sorry." Joy Anne and the other members of the Prophets' cult had been convinced that their actions were righteous too. *Two years old.* She suppressed a shudder. "We do the best we can to stop them." Ellie had decided that regardless of her curiosity, she couldn't afford to have this conversation in depth at the moment. They had to focus on the case.

"Thanks. And you're right, we will stop whoever is behind this. You have a great team here. It's easy to tell from the way you work together."

"Thank you." She assumed that Ann didn't want to deepen the subject either, as she moved on to another topic.

"I used to think it was like that for us. But I lost someone I loved to work with, and another cop in my unit just resigned. I guess I'm feeling nostalgic."

"Nothing wrong with that. We've gone through some changes as well," Ellie pointed out.

"Yeah. I guess that's inevitable."

"It is. Now let's see what Ms. Walton has to tell us."

Ellie didn't have much time to get nervous because of her surroundings. Annie Walton was eager to share her story. The prison guard had set up a room for them. Walton started talking the moment Ellie and Ann walked inside.

"I'm so glad you're here, and that someone will finally listen to me. Oh God, I was young and naïve, and there was no one left to blame but me. I don't think anyone ever believed the story."

"Well, you have a chance to tell it now," Ellie said to the woman in her early thirties. "The man you sold the drugs to, what was his name?"

"Davy," Annie said without hesitation. "I'm pretty sure that wasn't his real name."

"Did he look anything like this?"

She studied the composite critically and shrugged. Ellie's hope vanished.

"Close enough, I guess? This guy here looks older. He resurfaced?"

"Did he ever tell you what he was using the drugs for?"

"No, and I didn't ask. Like I said, I was naïve. He was nice to me, and he said he needed them. For what, I have no idea, but he did pay me. And then, all of a sudden, he was gone and as a parting gift, he ratted me out to my boss."

"How do you know it was him?" Ann asked the question that was on Ellie's mind.

"Because they told me a guy named Davy had called them to watch out for missing narcotics. The last time, they caught me, but he was long gone. So were the drugs, and eventually they thought it was my idea all along. Even my lawyer didn't believe me…Here we are."

"Do you remember anything else about him?"

"He said he worked in medical technology research…something about prosthetics, I think. But I guess that was a lie too. I've thought about this so many times, those words come back to taunt me. There was a facility in the area, but no Davy. If they ever checked that at all."

"Thank you, Ms. Walton, that's very helpful. Could you take a look at this picture?" A print had to do once more since she couldn't bring her phone in.

"That looks like him." Annie Walton studied the copy of Salter's photo, squinting.

"Are you sure?"

"Sort of. I don't know. I told you he was younger, better-looking back then."

"Okay. Thanks again."

"Hey," the woman called when they were already by the door. "If you find him, does that mean I'll get out of here?"

Ellie noticed Ann's wry smile. The woman seemed to have forgotten that even if they found "Davy," it would still be her who had stolen the drugs, because he told her he needed them. She wasn't sure what she could say without sounding patronizing.

"That's for the court to decide. Thank you for your time."

"Can you believe her?" Ann asked, dumbfounded, when they made their way back to the lockers where they'd left their cell phone and coats. "She barely knows him and clears out the shelves for this guy? Talk about desperate. And she thinks she's blameless."

"Yeah. Look, I need to check something. Remember what I told you about Eric Salter? He works in medical research. That all seems like a big coincidence."

"You're planning on bringing him in?"

"We'll ask him nicely, first thing in the morning," Ellie said.

Ellie had asked nicely. A disgruntled Eric Salter muttered about not having finished breakfast but agreed to join them at the station in order to answer more questions.

She and Ann joined Jordan, Derek, A.D.A. Esposito, and Lieutenant Carroll in the briefing room.

"Remember, so far we know that he *could* be the guy in the composite, and he *could* be someone who told Walton to steal drugs," he warned them.

"The person who killed Salter knows his way around drugs," Jordan said. "Same goes for Ashton Mayfield's killer. They might be one and the same after all. Wanting to getting rid of the competition? I'll be careful," she felt the need to add.

"I know you will be. All right. Let's get this started."

Jordan and Derek stepped into the room where Eric Salter sat at the table, his irritation palpable.

"I did what I could to help you," he greeted them. "Now why am I here again?"

"Do you know someone named Annie Walton?"

His expression was impassive. "Should I? The name doesn't ring a bell, but I've met many people over the years."

Jordan found it interesting that he didn't flat out deny the idea.

"She does seem to know you. Annie Walton is currently serving a prison sentence for possession and theft of drugs from her employer."

"That's too bad for her, but I still don't understand what this has to do with me."

"She says you asked her to steal them." That was stretching the truth a bit, but it had to do. Ashton Mayfield had been drugged, according to Dr. Adams.

"That's preposterous. You take the word of an inmate and drug addict over mine? I have an alibi!"

"For the night your father was murdered, yes. Where were you the following Friday?"

"At home. Alone. What, now you want to pin something else on me? I thought you caught my father's killer."

"We're not pinning anything on you," Derek reassured him. "Could you tell us a bit more about what you do at your job?"

He shrugged. "I told you, I do a bit of this and that, inventory and such. I don't handle any substances you need a special license for. I never finished medical school, remember? I know a little, and I work fast, so they hired me. That's it. I also do deliveries sometimes."

"Blood samples?"

"That's oddly specific," he said, and, out of the blue, smiled.

A chill ran down Jordan's spine, not because of him, or the present situation, but because something about his demeanor was familiar.

"Isn't it?" she agreed.

"This is all very interesting, but unless you're going to charge me with something, I want to talk to a lawyer. You can't hold me."

"Your father was a bad man, Eric. You told us so yourself."

"No argument from me, but I didn't kill him. Or anyone else."

"When did you first find out about what he was doing?" She perched on the edge of the table. "Did you tell anyone?"

He didn't move.

"I don't know what you're talking about. I want my lawyer, now."

"There's a very small window for you here," Jordan informed him. "If we find Tim Caplan alive, we'll consider that a sign of good will."

"Good luck with that." He started to laugh, startling her. "You're all grasping at straws. It would be funny if it wasn't so pathetic. About that phone call."

Jordan slipped off the table and went to the door.

"Not necessary. You're free to go."

He'd certainly assume that he'd be under surveillance, so they had to be extra careful.

Chapter Fourteen

A.D.A. Esposito, who had watched from behind the two-way mirror, looked doubtful.

"I won't deny there's something off about him, but the same thing could be said about many people, and I can't charge them. You didn't get a clear ID from Mulveney or Walton. I need a little more than that."

"Come on, Val. He's clever. He knows the area. I'm sure he knows what his father did, and he had means and opportunity—more than Cordell, actually," Jordan said. "He knows the system, so maybe he didn't steal any blood samples, he just exchanged them."

"Still not enough. It's all circumstantial. Adding up, for sure, but you've got to work on motive. Why would he want to reproduce his father's killings?"

"To punish them. To punish himself. Continue the family business, what do you think?"

Valerie raised an eyebrow, and Jordan realized her tone might not have been entirely appropriate. In the resulting silence, she admitted that she was glad to have at least one person in the room who didn't know the complicated history she had with another self-proclaimed "punisher." If Ann McCoy's curious expression was any indication, she hadn't done her research that far back, though according to Ellie, she knew about the Prophets case.

"In Salter's mind, being gay is a terrible thing punishable by death, and he passes that idea on to his son. Any attraction he might feel toward other men, he projects that on his victims, like father, like son."

"There might be another dimension to it, if some of the victims were underage," McCoy remarked. "Either one of them could be a pedophile."

"The thought had occurred to me," Jordan said, not hiding her frustration. "We know who's going to have a field day muddying the waters as usual. Walt Granger's father finds nothing wrong with calling gay people predators in general, and there are too many people like that, willfully ignorant or with an agenda."

Ellie shrugged. "Then we need to be very precise with the terms we use. That's all we can do."

It didn't seem enough. Days like this, nothing ever felt like it was enough.

Meanwhile, Tim Caplan was still out there.

"We'll do that. Let's bring the night shift up to date, and we'll call it a day."

It was a little late for Meri to still be up, but Jordan needed a moment to reassure herself. She had no illusions when it came to the extent of evil that drove some people. Jordan knew this kind of darkness intimately—and she would do whatever possible to keep Meri far away from it.

Jordan used to think that with Darby's death it would all be in the past, and to some extent, it had given her closure. But it was impossible to completely extinguish the harmful ideas, in everyday people, in psychopaths like him.

Meri, undisturbed by her thoughts, fell asleep in her arms even with all the conversations going on around her.

Jack and Pauline were still here. Derek, Kate, Maria, and Ann had joined them as well.

Jordan wondered if their reluctance to let go for only a few hours was borne out of a need to better the world, serve the public, or an addiction to adrenaline.

Perhaps all of the above.

"I'm sorry," she said. "I think someone needs to go to bed." Ann gave her a smile while everyone else was still engaged in their conversations.

Ellie followed her upstairs.

"I'm not sure, but I assume all those people expect some food. Is pizza okay with you?"

"Of course. Would you take care of that?"

"Sure." Ellie stepped forward and kissed her.

"What was that for?"

Given her earlier thoughts, Jordan almost expected some philosophical reasoning. Instead, Ellie said, "A preview for later, after we get everyone to leave."

No matter how dark the world got, it was always lighter because of Ellie in her life.

This connection had helped her survive under the worst of circumstances, at a time when they barely knew each other. She hoped that Tim Caplan had something equally as strong to hold on to.

❦

Jack and Pauline said goodbye to everyone, and Ellie got up to see them out. When they were at the door, Pauline turned.

"Oh, I forgot. I signed for a package that came for you earlier."

"Thank you. I'm not sure what it could be. Jordan!" Ellie called as she inspected the small package Pauline had deposited on a side table. Given their profession and experiences, it could be easy to become paranoid, but their friends had given them a lot of gifts for Meri. Noticing the logo of a local toy store, she opened the square package.

Jordan arrived, asking, "What's the emergency?" just as Ellie revealed the baby toy, a stuffed duckling made from soft fabric.

There was a printed note with the offering: *Sorry I'm late. Congratulations.*

"It would help if they'd signed it," Jordan said with a frown. "It's not that obvious who sent this."

"Well, we'll figure it out." Ellie didn't want to speculate about all the possibilities in front of her parents-in-law, though she assumed Jordan was thinking the same thing. If they couldn't trace it to anyone they knew, perhaps the toy should be analyzed for prints. For sure, they wouldn't give it to Meri right away. "It's cute," she said after they'd closed the door behind Jack and Pauline. "Maybe someone tried to be nice, and we're too inclined to see the worst in everyone."

Jordan sighed. "For a good reason. All right. Let's find out more first. We could drive by the store before work."

"Sounds like a plan."

They went back to the living room where Derek and Kate still sat talking.

"Before you ask, that wasn't either of us," Kate said with regard to the toy. "You know we like to take credit when Meri reacts all happy."

"I'd say it was one of our more humble friends, but we don't have any of those," Jordan said dryly.

"Better be safe than sorry. If you don't know where it came from, take it to the lab tomorrow."

Jordan didn't argue with Derek's statement.

Ellie was sure she would have preferred to think of the idea as paranoid, rather than a reasonable suggestion. This was the world they were living in.

"Speaking of which, is it okay if we call it a night? Sorry, Kate."

"No problem. I think we still have plans?" Kate and Derek shared a smile.

"Too much information. And remember, if something happens with Salter, we could get that call at any time."

"I am aware," Derek said. "Good night, everyone."

The call never came, and so the first task after a quick, too early breakfast, was a trip to BabyWorld. The employee looked skeptical when Ellie laid out their question.

"This looks like it was ordered online. You can add a personalized note, but there's no obligation to sign it."

"But you need an account? With a home address?"

"Any other information, I'd need a warrant."

Ellie cast a look at her watch. "I think we'll have to get back to you. Thanks anyway."

When they were back in the car, she voiced her thoughts out loud. "Are we losing our minds? Someone sent a toy for Meri, and they forgot to sign it."

"Or someone wants to mess with us, or worse, harm her. You heard Derek yesterday. I'm not taking any chances."

"I agree," Ellie said, though she still wasn't sure how she felt about this outcome. She thought of Ann McCoy's earlier revelation when she talked about the kidnapping of her niece. Somehow, it didn't feel right to keep that conversation from Jordan though she hadn't done it on purpose. They couldn't be too careful. What if someone had set their eyes on Meri? "Let's see what we can find out, but first...there's something else I have to tell you."

Jordan listened calmly when Ellie related what little information Ann McCoy had given her.

"Not that I think it's related or anything...but we always have to remember—"

"That there are awful people out there? Sorry. Go on."

"Well, I was going to say something along those lines," Ellie admitted. "She didn't say much, but it was clearly devastating."

Jordan nodded. "I don't even want to imagine. Let's make sure we didn't overlook anything."

At a red light, she took Ellie's hand. She hadn't realized how fast her heart had been beating until it slowly calmed.

The girl, Ariel, was there again, waiting for her companion. He wouldn't be joining her today to complain about his teammates, his parents, or the unjust world in general.

He had found a new friend.

Or, one could say, that friend had found him.

He loved the beginnings of new friendships, so much potential, so much time to learn, and accept the inevitable. Wondering when they'd start to bore him, and if he'd ever find the one.

It was downright crazy to come back here, but for some reason, he'd wanted to see her, the disappointment on her face. Strange to think that even after he'd invited his new friend, she still held his attention.

Maybe this was the beginning of the change he'd been waiting for.

It was finally working.

He slipped past the unmarked police car, back into his building, and came out as the person they were keeping tabs on. He'd go to work, come back, stay in for a while.

Too bad that his friends were going to miss a couple of meals, but that wasn't his fault. He couldn't take the chance.

❧

No one at the station thought that Jordan and Ellie were paranoid for taking the unexpected gift to the lab. That in itself was disconcerting.

"I could think of someone," Maria said. "It would fit his M.O., but as it is, the fish have probably eaten him by now."

Ellie's stomach churned at the image. "Did you have to say that?"

"It's true. If he'd survived that jump, we would have found him. But he liked to send Jordan things."

Noah Shriver, formerly a detective with Major Crimes, had murdered a sex worker and the owner of a strip club. He had also taken a liking to Jordan, followed her around, completely ignored the fact that she had a wife and a daughter.

"Like you said, there's no way he could have made it out of the river. Let's not do this. Excuse me," Ellie said when her cell phone rang. She answered without checking the caller ID, and at first, she had trouble to make out words.

"Ariel? What happened? Where are you?"

"I'm okay," Ariel said, and Ellie sighed in relief.

"Okay. Slow down, please. What's going on?"

"It's Owen. He hasn't come to school all week. His parents are only now going to the police."

Ellie remembered Ariel telling them about the young man she had befriended. At first, their friendship had raised suspicions until they learned about what connected them.

"I'm so sorry, Ariel. I'll see what I can find out, and as soon as we find him, you'll know too, okay? Where are you?"

"At school," Ariel said. "I'm scared for him. I read things online..."

"Please, don't do that. We don't know what happened," Ellie told her firmly. "I promise you I'll keep you up to date, but for now, stay where you are, and go straight home after school. One more thing, could you tell me Owen's last name?"

"It's Reed." Ariel sounded close to tears. "I have to go, class is starting. Please find him."

"We will," Ellie said before she ended the call. Once Ariel couldn't hear her anymore, she had different words. "Damn it!"

When Jordan mentioned Caplan, did Eric Salter laugh in their faces because he'd already found his next victim? Did that mean Tim Caplan was dead?

Chapter Fifteen

A nother family, another conflicted relationship between son and parents. Jordan had no time to obsess about the mysterious toy and or its sender's motivations.

"I didn't know!" Owen Reed's father claimed. "He said he was going to stay with a friend for a few days, a teammate. I thought...Well, that's not important right now. We fought about it, and he left. We found out only today that he never arrived there."

"The school didn't contact you?" Jordan asked.

"He's nineteen, no, they didn't contact us."

"Why didn't you want Owen to stay with that teammate?"

Jordan had caught Derek's warning glance. She wasn't about to go down that same road. It didn't mean she was going to spare them when it came to information they needed.

"We thought that..." Mr. Reed let his words trail off. Mrs. Reed looked away. "Anyway, so you've figured that out by now. Owen told us he was gay a few weeks ago, and obviously, we needed a moment to deal with that. He accused us of being homophobes. He also said he wanted to leave the dorm to live with one of the guys from his team."

Jordan remembered Ariel telling them that the teammates, too, had been somewhat reluctant. It was a silver lining to hear that not all of them rejected him—or that the Reeds might not be in the exact same category as the other parents they'd met. Still.

"His boyfriend?"

"Detective, that's inappropriate."

"I'm sorry, but we have to ask," she said softly. "We need to trace Owen's steps before he disappeared."

"I get that." Mr. Reed's exasperation had vanished. "I was afraid it might be the case, but they claimed they were just friends. I can give you his address."

"That would be helpful, thank you."

The college Owen Reed and his teammate Russell attended shared facilities with Ariel's high school, which was why she and Owen had met in the first place.

"Admit it, for a moment you were worried in there," Jordan said when they were en route to the campus.

"I wasn't. You know more than any of us what's at stake."

"Yeah, maybe. Yet, I'm naïve enough to hope that Owen is hiding out with that guy, because they want to run away together."

"I don't know if that's naïve," Derek said. "Human, maybe."

Russell was in class when they arrived, leaving the room under the curious glances of the other students. He destroyed their hopes quickly when they went to the student cafeteria.

"We weren't really that close," he said, "but I know he had some arguments with his parents, and he needed a break. He was going to pay his share of the rent."

"You never checked in with him after he didn't show up?"

He shrugged. "I assumed he changed his mind. But then his dad called…and you know the rest. No one knew where he was, so they called the police."

"Do you know if Owen met anyone new lately?" At this point, Jordan had trouble hiding her frustration. Not that it was anything new or surprising. Few people paid attention to what was going on around them. In her early school years, no one had any idea of what her home life looked like. For years, no one asked.

"I know that he was always chatting with one of those girls from the high school team. I thought it was odd since she was so much younger than him, but of course he wasn't interested in her that way."

"Was he interested in you?"

"If he was, he never told me, and I sure wasn't."

Russell's face reddened, which could mean a multitude of things. But Jordan believed that he had no idea where Owen was, which effectively killed her best-case scenario.

"All right. One more thing. Have you ever seen this man? Hanging around the school maybe, or at games?"

Jordan slid her phone over to him, and he studied the picture of Eric Salter closely.

"Never seen him."

"Thank you, Russell. If you can think of anything else, please call."

"Sure thing," he said.

That, Jordan wasn't sure she could believe.

❧

Another day went by. Once again, the surveillance of Eric Salter yielded nothing out of the ordinary: He went to work and back and stayed in for the night. A waste of time? Jordan was aware that it might be too early to tell, but they didn't have a lot of time to prevent another murder.

The press was covering the disappearances, though when the Mayfields came onto the screen, accusing the police of not doing their job, Jordan turned off the TV.

That night, Lieutenant Carroll sent them home with a sobering message.

"There'll be a press conference on Monday morning. I need to give the people something to contradict the idea that we're sitting around doing nothing here. Make sure I can."

That night, they had dinner with only Kate and Derek. While Kate and Ellie got Meri to bed, Jordan realized that Derek had gone out onto the porch. She picked up her bottle and followed him outside. The night was chilly, but bearable.

"I'm sorry your theory didn't work out," he said.

"Yeah, me too. We're not giving these kids enough stories with a happy outcome."

"To run away with the boyfriend?"

"Better than being sent to a conversion camp. Though that still beats being kidnapped by a serial killer."

"Yeah. Tough to think of a happy outcome when people are...people."

Jordan recalled the conversation they'd had right after her lapse of reason.

"You know that cop who pulled you over for some bullshit reason..."

"Leave it alone, Jordan," he said with surprising heat.

"I don't know if that's a good idea."

"You don't know everything."

"Walters is out, but we all tolerated his crap for too long—until he actually committed a crime. I really hate it that Atwood still has a job at the department."

"What's your point? Claiming an honest mistake usually works. The blue wall holds."

"This is not okay. We need to have each other's backs out there, but we can't reward bad behavior."

Derek sat his bottle on the railing. "And there's a limit as to what we can do against it. Carroll knows. And you know he has to keep the politics in mind, just like he did when he promised the Mayfields an apology from you."

Jordan let that information sink in, shaking her head even as she couldn't find the words to contradict Derek's statement. Perhaps she'd been naïve at one point but not about wanting to give Owen Reed and others a happy ending. She hated not having an answer.

At least, they knew where they stood with each other. For the moment, it had to be enough, even though it wasn't in the bigger context.

"You heard anything about the toy?" he asked after a few seconds of silence.

"Not yet. I would have told you."

"It might still be nothing."

Jordan appreciated the sentiment though she could tell he wasn't convinced.

⸎

The next day, Jordan and Ellie went to see Ariel again. Unfortunately, she had nothing to add to her initial statement.

"We talked a lot about dreams, where we would like to go? When I meet people, a lot of the time, they have heard my name, and the story about the Prophets. Owen wanted to start over somewhere, where no one would judge him."

"His parents were still talking to him though."

Ariel shrugged. "Yes. I guess they were making an effort."

"Ariel, did you ever see this man talk to Owen, or hang out anywhere near your school?"

"He looks like the delivery guy. I think I saw him with the school nurse once?"

Why wasn't anybody ever sure about him?

Jordan suppressed a sigh. "Thank you."

"Thank you both for coming. Jordan, can I speak with you for a moment?" Ellie stayed with Ariel while Jordan followed Becca Crane, Ariel's aunt, into the living room.

"Is that the man you suspect to be the kidnapper?"

"I'm sorry, I can't talk about an ongoing investigation," Jordan said automatically, flinching when Becca said, "Bullshit. There's a reason why you asked me to basically keep Ariel grounded, and you ask her about this man…You think she's in danger from him?"

"I don't think so. That's not the kidnapper's M.O. But she was close with Owen, so I have to make sure if she knows something, we'll know it too."

Becca sighed. "I'm sorry for going off on you like this, but she could really do without having this much attention from the police and press again. What is it with parents freaking out over their gay kids anyway? I want mine to be happy and healthy."

"You met his parents?"

"Of course. We talked about this. When I realized Ariel was chatting with a nineteen-year-old, I had to make sure that there was nothing inappropriate going on. But…He was lonely. I guess in a way, she still is, no matter what we do, and if they understood each other, I didn't want to be in the way. I hope he's okay."

"Yeah, so do we. What about the picture? You think she could be right about the delivery guy? That actually is part of the man's job."

"Show it to me again?"

Becca looked at the photograph and shrugged. "I'm afraid he's not that memorable, but Ariel has good memory."

Not that memorable was the best-case scenario for someone who wanted to go unnoticed, Jordan thought.

If that was Eric Salter's intention, he had certainly succeeded for far.

Derek had made a coffee and donut run before they reconvened at the station, earning everyone's gratitude.

"Okay. Ariel Deane. What's your theory here?" he asked Jordan.

"There's no theory. It's a coincidence she and Owen became friends. She doesn't know anything that could put her in danger."

"You don't sound convinced."

"I'm not," Jordan confessed. "It's too close for comfort, and she's already been through so much. I don't want to leave anything up to chance."

"What does that mean?" Ann asked. "If his M.O. is the same as his father's, wouldn't he stick to one gender? And if he doesn't, should we assume he's—"

"Psychopath is not a sexual orientation," Maria Doss said. "That's what he is if he kidnapped and killed these men."

"I didn't mean..."

"I know." Maria sighed. "Everyone's on edge. You got anything on that toy yet?"

"As a matter of fact, I do." Everyone turned to Dr. Adams who had joined them.

"Please, make it quick." Jordan muttered.

"I'm sorry, but you're not going to like this. There were prints on the package and the toy, and...surprise. Dead man walking."

"You've got to be kidding me."

"Sorry, I'm not. Just when I told you it was Mr. Cordell's blood on that branch."

"No, no, this can't be true." At this point Jordan didn't care much who was listening. "I can't believe he's that stupid. He gets away from the police for this long, and that's what he does?"

Ellie looked frustrated as well. Jordan could only imagine what was on her mind.

"Guess my case just broke wide open. We better get in touch with Lieutenant Daniels," she said. Daniels had been Shriver's boss at Major Crimes.

"Meanwhile, with all the media attention, we're still letting Salter string us along, and nothing on Caplan and Reed."

"Sorry." Dr. Adams held up her hands before she snatched a plate and a donut. "Don't kill the messenger."

Later that day, James McKenzie called her and asked for a meeting.

"If this is about Cordell...I'm not quite ready to call Occam's Razor into question, but there is likely something more to the story, I'll give you that. Can it be tomorrow?"

"You might want it today. I have a story about your alternative suspect, Salter."

"How did you—never mind. Just come on over. Ellie or I will be here unless something big happens. Care to give me a preview?"

"I'm happy to. First of all, would you let Ellie know I'm now representing Annie Walton? There are a few elements that convinced me her case should be reopened."

"You're a dreamer," she said, aware that she sounded a tad jealous. There were times when she did envy Ellie for her relentless optimism, much as it eased her own mind. James McKenzie took near impossible cases for similar reasons.

"Oh, but this is real. Wait until I can show you. It looks like Mr. Salter didn't randomly decide to quit medical school. There was an incident with an underage girl. The family moved away, and I haven't been able to locate them yet...but something is seriously wrong there."

"I'd say so. All right. I'll wait for you."

Ariel hadn't been able to concentrate all day. Usually, the structure of school and training had been the comfort that allowed her to settle into life after the Prophets, after losing her mother. Until Joy Anne and her crazed act. Now, Owen was missing. His parents were on TV almost every day, blaming the police like the other couple that she'd seen in the news. They had abandoned their son Ashton a long time ago. Owen's parents hadn't noticed he wasn't in school.

She felt constantly on alert, the way it had been when she was still living on the compound. Like something horrible could happen at any moment—that wasn't an irrational fear, but experience.

She wanted to be like her classmates, like other teenagers, but this was what separated her from most of them.

One day, she'd walked past a group of college athletes, sensing that they were talking about her. She knew for sure when it was Owen who shut them up, and the next time she saw him, he apologized for something that wasn't even his fault. His parents hadn't locked him up and for sure, they weren't murderers, though some of their views weren't so different from those of the Prophets.

All of this was on her mind every minute of the day now, robbing her of sleep at night. She had been reading the same text three times and still couldn't make sense of it as she sat at her desk, trying to focus on her homework while the world was going to hell again.

About that part, the Prophets might have been right, but they were completely wrong and ignorant about who was to blame for it.

She jumped when her cell phone vibrated on the table. Grateful for the distraction, she picked it up, her heart beating faster when she realized that the text came from Owen.

-Hi A., I just wanted to tell you I'm ok. Thank you for listening. Please don't tell anyone I contacted you.

Ariel stared at the words for a full minute, wishing they could be true. Maybe he just needed to get away from it all? He had to know that the police were looking for him.

-Where are you? she typed but didn't send the text. She deleted it and started over. *I'm glad. But you should call your parents.*

-I can't, the answer came right away. *You know how they are.*

-I'm sorry.

A few minutes passed by, and she was scared she might have lost him.

-Could we meet? Ariel waited, pressing her fingernails into her palm so hard she was breaking skin.

Then, finally, she had her answer.

Chapter Sixteen

As it turned out, Jordan wasn't going to stay at the station to wait for McKenzie: The uniformed officers on Salter's tail, Lyons and Atwood, informed them that he was on the move, leaving city limits.

"All right, we'll catch up to them. You wait here for James?"

Ellie nodded. Detective McCoy was on her feet in a heartbeat.

"I'd prefer if you stay here," Jordan told her. "We don't even know if he's going to lead us to Caplan or Reed, but if he does, we don't want to tip him off."

"I understand," Ann said, though she clearly didn't agree.

"Any sign of Tim, we'll let you know right away, I promise. Derek, come on."

They hurried to the car and were minutes later following the directions given to them by Officers Lyons and Atwood. Jordan didn't like that Atwood was a part of this, though Casey Lyons, a seasoned officer and a good friend, would be able to keep him in check if necessary. Salter was clever—they had no use for any surprises from one of their own. She still felt uneasy about the conversation she and Derek had the other day.

She wasn't even sure if she considered Atwood "one of their own" or if he did. In any case, they needed to focus on the task at hand.

They hadn't approached enough to see his car yet, but Atwood was confirming that he and Casey were still behind him. He had left the highway for a road leading to an industrial area. The officers had followed him onto the property of a large construction firm, where he turned and headed in the opposite direction.

"I'll be damned," Atwood said after a few tense minutes.

"What's going on?" Jordan asked.

"Looks like he's just driving up and down the perimeter."

"Did he notice you?"

"If he did, he's playing with us," Casey sounded frustrated. "Wait. He's stopping."

"Be careful," Jordan warned, rolling her eyes when she heard Atwood scoff. "Where are you?"

Casey described their exact location. Jordan and Derek would be able to cut off Salter's path from the direction they were coming from.

"Okay, we're almost there. Wait for us."

"He's entering the building."

"We're on the other side. Stay where you are."

Atwood grumbled something that prompted Casey to say sharply, "Not the time."

Jordan and Derek arrived on the other side of the building, where they parked the car.

"Okay. Let's see what Eric is up to."

⁂

Time went by without a message from Jordan and Derek, or James McKenzie showing up. Ann McCoy looked impatient, and Ellie couldn't blame her. At least the lieutenant had come back in when she notified him of Dr. Adams' findings. To her surprise, he brought Lt. Daniels with her.

"Harding, come with us?" he asked when they walked past her desk.

"I'm sorry," she whispered to Ann before getting to her feet. "Let me know when Mr. McKenzie arrives?"

"Sure."

Ellie hurried to keep up with Carroll and Daniels.

"Where's Carpenter?" he asked when the door of his office was closed.

"Out with Detective Henderson. Salter is on the move."

Carroll sighed, Daniels looked tense.

"Tell me again about that package."

"There's nothing I haven't told you before. It's a local toy store. Jordan's mom answered the door. We didn't see it until later that night. The message wasn't signed, so we took it to the lab." Ellie cringed a bit, still thinking it sounded paranoid—but it turned out they had a reason.

"No sign of life until now," Daniels said. "It's been half a year. He must have thought this was important. I want you to be careful."

There were certain implications to her words. Jordan wouldn't like them, and, Ellie suspected, neither would Carroll.

"I agree, but much as I'd like, with the tail on Salter, we don't have the budget for 24/7 protection."

"That's unfortunate," Daniels commented, and for the first time, Ellie noticed the tension between them.

"It is, but this is where we are."

"It's not Jordan's fault that he was kind of obsessed with her."

"You're stating the obvious, Harding. I still have the press conference to deal with. Find those missing men, and find Shriver, and much of this mess will be over."

Ellie found that pretty obvious too, but she kept her thoughts to herself.

"I'm waiting for Mr. McKenzie," she said instead. "He says he has new information on Salter."

"So where is he?"

Ellie cast a quick glance at her watch. "I don't know. I should go check again." To her relief, Carroll nodded, and she was able to escape the strange atmosphere.

Jordan and Derek caught up with Lyons and Atwood near the entrance of the warehouse.

Something about this set-up didn't feel right to her. Why would Salter drive around merrily before parking his car in a warehouse's lot? If he suspected the police of following him, he wouldn't lead them right to the scene of his crimes.

If he had been aware of his father's crimes, covered up for them or copied them, he was a lot smarter than that.

"What are we waiting for?" Atwood asked. "He's in there, only one entrance. We got him."

"On what?" Jordan asked. "Going into a warehouse? That might be trespassing at best."

"Or we find the victims before it's too late. Henderson, help me out here."

If it wasn't for the rather tense situation, Jordan might have laughed, and she could only imagine what was on Derek's mind. He and Atwood didn't often see eye to eye.

"Give it another moment."

"To do what?" Atwood seethed.

They heard sounds coming from behind a door, a high-pitched voice.

Jordan could swear Atwood was gloating, but she wasn't going to waste time arguing if they could save a life.

The door led to a staircase down some stairs into a hallway that abruptly ended with a black curtain. A burly man stepped outside, his hand going for his gun though he quickly thought twice when he realized who the unexpected guests where.

"What the hell is going on here?" Jordan asked, though she was aware that no one had the time to answer. Past the curtain, there were a number of rooms. In the second to the left she found Eric Salter with his pants down. The woman with him, a few years older than Salter from the looks of it, hastily covered himself. She didn't seem in immediate distress.

"Detective." He grinned. "You have a way of messing with my plans. Or is there something of interest here for you?"

She ignored whatever insinuation he might have wanted to make.

"Get dressed, and let's have a talk at the station."

"Oh, not that again. I paid this lady. Isn't that right?" The woman nodded.

Jordan could swear he was moving slowly on purpose. Part of her noted how different his demeanor was from the first few encounters. He had believably acted like she would have expected from someone who wasn't close with his family, and for a reason. Lately, his immediate incentive seemed to be pissing her off. He was succeeding, too.

"We'll sort all of this out at the station. I'm pretty sure none of what is happening here is legal, so...You might want to invite your lawyer to that conversation again."

This time, they might be able to hold him, though they still had nothing as to the location of Tim Salter and Owen Reed. Somehow, this didn't feel like a victory.

Jordan hoped that the real possibility of detainment would convince Salter to talk. Time was ticking, not just for the lieutenant's press conference, but two young men likely in mortal danger.

-I can't tell you much, but I would love to see you one last time. I can trust you, right?

-I swear you can. I won't tell anybody. Just tell me where you are, and I'll find a way to get there.

-Not even your aunt, okay?

-I promise.

-Okay. Wait until tonight...

Ellie sighed in relief when she received the short message from Jordan. This wasn't exactly the outcome they'd hoped for, but Eric Salter was finally implicated in something illegal. They had a certain window of time to get the information they needed.

With everything going on, she hadn't said anything to Jordan about her conversation with Carroll and Daniels, but she couldn't put it off forever. Shriver might not present an immediate danger—there was no certainty with someone who had already killed two people and had been willing to jump off a bridge to escape apprehension.

She didn't think he wanted to do Jordan harm, but they couldn't take that risk.

Ellie got up to check the interrogation rooms so everything would be ready once Salter and the other parties arrived. When she returned, she saw Libby Marshall heading towards her, her expression serious. Detective McCoy was with her.

"It's about the lawyer, McKenzie," she said.

"I just came from the hospital," Libby added. "Someone beat him up badly."

Ellie's hand went to her mouth. "Any idea...Did you speak to him?"

Libby shook her head. "Wes is still there in case...Doctors didn't want to give too many reassurances, but they think he'll make it. He has yet to wake up."

"That's terrible. Thank you though."

She was aware that Wes and Libby had made a judgment call, and that they would have called in a Homicide detective if they thought the situation could take an abrupt turn to the worse.

"I'd like to go anyway, see if I can learn anything," she said, turning to Ann. "Could you wait here for Jordan and Derek?"

"No problem."

The detective had resigned to the fact that this wasn't her turf.

"McKenzie wanted to talk to us about something Salter did as a young man, an incident that had him expelled from the university. I'm sure this is somehow related."

"Good luck," Ann said. "I'm sorry."

"Thanks. I'll talk to you later."

Chapter
Seventeen

E llie wasn't prepared for the wave of emotion hitting her when she walked into the waiting area, where she found McKenzie's husband Michael with a small group of their friends and family.

"I'm so sorry," she said, her breath catching in her throat. She forewent a formal greeting in favor of a quick hug. They didn't know each other well, but they had talked a few times at the *D&T*. Dan, one of the owners, was sitting in one of the seats as well. Ellie had to remind herself that she wasn't here to be another friendly face or confront one of her own worst memories. "I know you talked to the officers already, but could we sit for a moment?"

Michael looked uncertain.

An older woman, his mother judging from the resemblance, laid her hand on his shoulder. "Go. We'll come get you if there's anything new."

Ellie found a quieter waiting area. Neither of them felt like sitting down.

"Look, I know there's only one thing on your mind right now, but I do need your help. James was on his way to see me and Jordan with a story regarding a suspect. Does he ever talk to you about any of his cases?"

"Rarely. I mean, the guy who might have killed the serial murderer, yes, we talked about this briefly, but not so much about the client."

Ellie could imagine. Salter's story would strike terror in the heart of the community, just like Joy Anne Deane's act had.

"So, he mentioned Charles Salter. Did he say anything about his son, Eric?"

"No, like I said, it wasn't really about the work, but the sick old bigot," he said with disgust. "You know what's bizarre? These things always bring out those wingnuts. Most people are shocked, but a few of them will come out and say, hey, they had it coming. They think it's okay as long as the right people get hurt, and then...this happens."

Ellie knew he was at the end of his rope. She knew exactly how that felt. Forcing her own emotions aside, she asked, "Did you receive any threats?"

It could be random violence, it could be that Michael was right, and the repeated coverage of Salter's murders might have inspired a certain element to crawl out from whatever rock they'd been hiding under. All of it was possible, though the connection to Salter junior was too much of a coincidence. Except Eric had led the police on a wild goose chase tonight—he didn't have time, did he?

On the other hand, Jordan had talked to James just hours before Casey and Atwood notified them that Eric was on the move.

He could have paid someone.

Michael shrugged as if the question had only now registered with him.

"He's a public defender. People get angry sometimes, but nothing like this. Maybe we've been fooling ourselves."

"What about today? Was there anything out of the ordinary?"

"I would tell you if I knew," he said, frustrated. "I told the officers everything already. This is going nowhere, right?"

"Why would you say that?"

"Like that guy Jerry who hangs out at the *D&T*? Did you ever find who beat him that night?"

Ellie was ashamed to acknowledge that she knew what case he was talking about, and that they'd never found the attacker.

"That's what I thought."

"Hey. Listen. The case is still open. We're not going to let this go. I promise."

She couldn't blame him for looking doubtful.

"I have to go now. We're all rooting for James."

"He's going to make it, right? He has to."

"He will," Ellie said, her voice as firm as she hoped it would be. She accompanied him back to the other waiting room and left. Ellie felt like she was moving underwater as she walked along the hallways to the front door, and to her car in the parking lot. She sat behind the wheel, started the engine, and turned it off as tears clouded her vision.

⁂

"So far, we have solicitation, illegal possession of a firearm, and a little extra for Narcotics," Derek said as he joined Jordan in the observation area.

She took a sip of her coffee she'd just refilled, wincing at the burn.

"Nothing regarding Caplan and Reed."

"Not yet. The people we talked to at the warehouse swear they don't know anything about the kidnappings. It's possible that Salter was trying to create a false trail."

"And get himself arrested in the process? That doesn't make sense."

"Well, let's ask him."

"Sure. You'll be the bad cop. Let's confuse him a little, maybe that will help."

Derek shook his head, but he went inside the interrogation area ahead of her.

Jordan closed the door and leaned against the wall, sipping the coffee, watching as Derek tossed the file he'd brought with him, on the table. He let the chair scrape over the floor before he sat down.

Eric Salter looked right past him at Jordan.

"You're trying to stare me down or what? I'm beginning to think you want to drag me in here every once in a while, just because you can." He leaned back in his seat. "You liked what you saw earlier, Detective?"

"You can play these stupid games, and the next one to get a glimpse will be a prison guard, or you can work with us," Derek informed him. "Right now, you're in big trouble. That window my colleague told you about the other time, it's closed."

"Oh, you think so? Yet, you're no closer to proving I had anything to do with those boys' disappearances."

"See, that's where you're mistaken. We spoke to Mr. McKenzie who had a lot of interesting things to say about your conduct in medical school."

Jordan noticed with satisfaction that he blanched at the suggestion. She stepped closer.

"Look, the deal we were talking about the other day is off, given the fact that you assaulted a public defender, not to mention that old story that came back to haunt you. There's a pattern here, Eric, and it's getting harder and harder to deny. The best you can do for yourself is to come clean right this moment. You might even find a sympathetic judge...Because I think your father started the killings at a time when you had no way of stopping him."

Salter stared at her as if she'd said something utterly grotesque.

"Of course I had no way of stopping him, what do you think? There were always rumors, as long as I can remember. Some people said that he was cheating on my mother, and that only made him angrier."

Jordan sat across from him, leaning forward.

"When did you first find out?"

He raked a hand through his hair, looking alarmed all of a sudden. She wasn't sure what to make of it. Was he having a flashback? Was this all an act?

"Eric. Please. Talk to me."

He laughed nervously. "At some point I figured it out that they didn't want to be there. Should have bought a clue, right? Who would want to be with Charles Salter? But no one had a choice in the matter. If it wasn't them, he would have killed me and my mother. That's all I can tell you."

Jordan kept her impression impassive, nothing in her posture revealing her inner turmoil. She knew there was a lot more to the story.

"So, you knew what he was doing. You maybe even spoke to one of the victims?"

Next to her, Derek sat with his back straight. He was likely thinking the same thing.

"Did he ever make you take part in the murders?"

She had to move carefully, but at the same time, they didn't have a moment to waste.

"He said I could never leave."

Jordan couldn't help flinching when he started laughing.

"Showed him, didn't I? It took me some time to figure out that he wasn't going to tell on me, because I could tell on him just as easily. I moved away and tried to forget about it all."

A psychiatrist would be helpful to sort out the details, but Jordan could see the gruesome picture unfold. Eric Salter had never forgotten about his father's crimes. At one point, the compulsion to replicate them had likely taken over.

Before or after Charles Salter's death? When Eric came to visit his father, did he witness any crimes? Participate in them? What had really happened to Mrs. Salter?

All of these questions were relevant, but there was another one that superseded them by far.

"But you couldn't, right? You tried to get rid of the memories and the monster, but that didn't work out."

"I had to stop him, don't you understand? That was the only way."

"Tell us where Owen Reed and Tim Caplan are."

"I don't know! I stopped a serial killer, doesn't that count for anything?"

It took every last bit of self-restraint not to throw it back in his face. He was hardly a hero. An innocent man had nearly gone to prison, and he had assaulted a witness. They'd have to deal with that later.

"It could mean that you don't have to serve your sentence in the general population where some inmates might be aware of your crimes."

"Wow, detective, that's a low blow." His laughter was jarring, the instant switch of gears giving Jordan whiplash. "You're suggesting someone might want to hurt me after everything I went through? Just because you can't find those boys?"

"I see we're not getting anywhere. We have you on a number of felonies, and you just told us you were aware of your father's crimes. Maybe after you've stared at the inside of a prison cell long enough, you'll change your mind."

Both she and Derek got up to walk to the door.

"Detective Carpenter."

When they turned around, he said, "I have something for you. Just you."

Derek shook his head, but she walked closer anyway, though not within his reach. She had to lean forward to hear Salter whisper, "You lock me up, and those boys are going to die."

"You keep stalling, and we might not be able to guarantee your safety," she returned, already knowing it wouldn't have the desired effect. Jordan was more than eager to leave the room, if only for a few minutes.

"Damn, he's a piece of work," she commented as soon as they were in the observation area. "What are the chances Mrs. Salter didn't die of natural causes?"

"I'd say they're pretty high." Derek sounded as frustrated as she felt. "Anything from Ellie?

Checking her cell phone, Jordan said, "She's on the way here. Let's go back to that board for a moment. This many crimes, there are receipts somewhere."

On their way to the briefing room, she saw Ellie sitting at her desk.

"Hey. Are you coming with us?"

"Sure."

When she got up, Jordan noticed she looked pale and tired. "I need good news," she told her as they were walking. "Derek just told Salter that we talked to James."

With a sigh, Ellie said, "Well, that story hasn't become any more likely, at least as far as I know. There was no change when

151

I left. Wes will stay for the time being, and he'll call as soon as we can see James."

Jordan wished she had anything encouraging to tell her. As it was, they were still racing against the clock.

"Okay. It would make sense if Salter is behind this, but how did he pull that off?"

"He paid someone?" Derek suggested.

"That's one explanation, though I can't see him trusting someone else with the job. And here we are," she said when they were standing in front of the board after Ellie had closed the door. "We assume that Salter got away with switching the blood samples. Since the blood on the branch matched the sample the clinic had on file, this worked for a while. He killed his father...Why? The threat of exposing one another had been hanging over their heads for many years. Why now?"

She'd been so immersed in the question she hadn't heard the door open again.

"I know I'm late to the party, but I have some ideas if you'd like to hear them."

For years, Jordan had been unhappy when Dr. Bethany Roberts swooped in on a case, but she was more than willing to admit that they needed the help.

Behind her, Ann McCoy entered the room.

"I'm sorry to interrupt, but I had a call from my boss," she said. "He was asking me about the arrest. I wanted to check with you before I get back to him."

❦

"You've done some great work here, so most of mine is to provide you with the science to back up your court case once you're there," Bethany said. "I don't expect you'll want to go into details with the missing persons cases still open, but I'm here for any questions. Everything Salter told you about his father is important, even though there might be some inconsistencies."

"He hated him, but he wanted to be like him? Because in Eric's mind, his father had all the power?"

Ellie might be tired, but her conclusions sounded spot on to Jordan. There was a missing piece in here somewhere. It intrigued her that Bethany mentioned the inconsistencies without having spoken to Eric Salter.

"Nevertheless. This all makes sense, but it doesn't help us with the urgent case."

"Maybe it will. I'd like to give it a go," Bethany insisted.

"Can't say no to that, can we?"

"Not really. Let's do this."

Chapter Eighteen

"I think I'll be okay," Bethany said when Jordan was about to go into the room with her. She nodded to Atwood who was guarding Salter. "If you could stay for a moment?" she asked him before she nearly closed the door in Jordan's face.

"What the hell is she up to?" Derek asked.

They watched from behind the glass as Salter cast an uncertain look at Atwood before he faced Bethany.

"I'm not dangerous," he claimed.

"I didn't think you were, Eric." Her tone was light, almost jarringly cheery, given the context.

"And who are you?"

"Dr. Bethany Roberts. I'm a psychiatrist with the FBI."

"What the hell?" he grumbled. "What makes you think I need a psychiatrist?"

"I know you've seen a few. And given what I've learned, you must have a lot on your mind."

"Well, yeah. Doesn't everybody?"

He cast another nervous glance at Chris Atwood.

"You told the police that the reason you killed your father was to stop him."

"Really, you're going to go over that again? You must have endless resources."

On the other side of the glass, Jordan couldn't help scoffing. Given what she'd learned from Ellie earlier, Lieutenant Carroll would hardly agree.

"The thing is I don't believe you." Bethany's pleasant tone belied the message. "I mean, why go to all the trouble to frame someone? You could have gone to the police, or if you were afraid to implicate yourself, give an anonymous tip. He would have had to answer for those bones in his basement anyway."

"He never had to answer to anyone. I think he had police in his pocket. I couldn't take the risk. I couldn't go to prison!"

"Because there was something else you had to take care of?"

"What do you mean?"

Bethany let him stew for almost over a minute. He started fidgeting.

"I think your father killed those men, because he hated them, because he hated himself. Those were the lessons you grew up with."

"He was the killer. I'm fine."

"Are you, Eric? Or had you gotten tired of sharing?"

He looked down at the table. "It's not that easy," he said.

Outside the room, Jordan was getting impatient. "No, no, we know this already. He's just going to realize we have nothing."

"Oh, it is easy. He was ruthless, pure evil. You waited many years for him to treat you as an equal, but he would have never done that. Is that why you escalated? Got careless? Because let me tell you, at the rate you're going, you'll never last as long as your father did."

He stared at her, unflinching.

"What if I already have?"

"I'm listening."

"Jordan, Ellie, there's someone here to talk to you."

Jordan turned to Libby Marshall. "Now's not a good time," she said. "I think he's going to—"

"It's Ariel Crane. She seems pretty upset." Ariel had taken the Crane's name after being formally adopted.

"I'll stay here," Derek said. "Go."

Standing by Ellie's desk, Ariel looked frightened. Her aunt was with her, the tension between the two of them palpable.

"Hi, Becca. Ariel, sweetie, what happened?"

"I think I know where Owen is," she said, holding out her cell phone. You need to trace this, now."

Ellie took the phone from her, scrolling through the messages on the screen.

"We will, I promise," she said, seeing the urgency. Her stomach was churning at what this could have meant. She handed the phone to Libby and instructed her to bring it to the tech lab right away, then she picked up the phone to call ahead. "Sit, please," she said after ending the call. "When did this happen?"

"Earlier. I was so happy to hear from him, and for a moment, I really thought we got it all wrong, that he just needed to get away, you know?"

Ellie didn't tell her what she already suspected. That Owen Reed wasn't safe somewhere, and he hadn't written that message. But how could Salter have pulled this off with everything else that was going on, ending in his arrest?

They'd have to make sure Ariel understood she should have told them anyway.

"I had no idea until she showed me those texts," Becca added. "We came here right away." Ellie suspected she had already addressed the possible consequences of Ariel's omission on the way.

"What changed your mind?" she asked.

Ariel shivered. "He sounded off to me, different from his other texts. I realized what that reminded me of. Every once in a while, someone at the Prophets got hold of a phone, Mom, Jennifer, and they were always speaking in code in case on of the brothers tried to recover the message."

Her eyes welled up. Ellie didn't have to ask. Ariel's mother was dead, and so was Jennifer Beaumont, a young woman who had infiltrated the cult in order to expose them in a book.

"I would have called you, I promise, but I read over the message again, and I got scared. I think someone has his phone, and...I wanted it to be true, because it meant he wasn't one of them."

One of them, the missing persons cases that were in the media all day, every day.

"I understand. It's good that you came. We'll try to locate the phone, and I'm sure that will help us find Owen. I need you both to go home now."

"Can't I stay here?"

"I'm afraid that's not possible," Jordan said. "We'll call as soon as we know more, I promise."

"He's my friend."

"Ariel," Becca chided.

"I understand. Let me walk you out. We'll talk later, okay?"

Reluctantly, Ariel obliged.

"I'm really sorry," Becca said.

"It's okay. We're taking care of it."

When Jordan returned, Ellie was still waiting in the same spot, absorbing what they'd learned. "Dear God. He was trying to lure her to wherever he is holding them."

"Ariel is safe. And he's not going anywhere. Come on. I think Bethany could use a break."

Ellie followed her, resigned to the fact that a part of this conversation had to wait until later. On the bright side, this new information increased their chances of finding Owen Reed alive.

Or were they deluding themselves?

When they returned to the observation area, Lieutenant Carroll was with Bethany.

"This isn't working," he remarked. "He's going back and forth between suggesting your theory is correct and trying to debunk it."

Bethany wasn't fazed by the implied criticism, if there was any.

"Yes, that's to be expected. I think we all agree that he witnessed some horrible acts at a fairly young age. How young, that's hard to determine, but there are definitely dissociative elements in his behavior."

"What, like a multiple personality disorder?" Jordan didn't mean to snap at her. She was already frustrated at what that might mean for Tim and Owen, and their case in general.

"No, not like that, I don't think so. He remembers what he did, understands what he did, and that it's wrong—and given what happened with the blood samples, he shows considerable effort to cover up the crimes. All I'm saying is that he's compartmentalizing a great deal more than the average person. Part of him still feels like the boy who couldn't say no to his father. I'd guess the initial incident happened sometime in his early teenage years, though we'd need a lot more time to determine that."

"And there are other parts, you think?"

"Not distinct personalities, but different states, if you will, yes. And one of them is that he feels invincible, superior to his father, and entitled to both punishing and owning those young men."

"Girls, too." Ellie looked like she was feeling sick at the image Bethany evoked. "There was the incident at his university. We'll get the notes from McKenzie's office by court order probably tomorrow. And he wrote the text messages from Owen Reed's phone."

"Where are we on this?" Carroll asked.

"Work in progress. The phone company understands that there's a life at stake, but there are still steps to take."

"Well, the Crane girl is safe for now, with Salter behind bars. Let's all keep it that way and find me where that damn phone is."

"Yes, sir," she said.

After the meeting dissolved, Jordan found Ann McCoy still in the briefing room, standing in front of the board, her gaze fixed on the picture of Tim Caplan.

"Once we find that phone, there's a good chance we'll find him too."

That was the limit as to how uplifting she could get at this time of the day. Ann understood that there was a good chance they'd find more dead bodies in a cave somewhere.

"You talked to your boss yet?"

"I'll call him tomorrow."

"Okay. You don't have to stay."

Ann shrugged. "It's not like I have anywhere to be. When we find Tim, I'll have a lot of calls to make."

"Sure. Speaking of which...I'll be right back."

Outside, she stepped into a corner to call Pauline, starting with an apology.

"We're both tied up here, I'm not sure for how long."

"That's fine. Everything is quiet here, and my replacement just arrived. Hang on."

A second later, Kate spoke, "Hey. Don't worry about anything. I can stay the night if necessary."

"Thank you so much, that's a relief."

"I'd have done it anyway, but I'm guessing Derek won't be coming home anytime soon?"

"Probably not. Things are moving. Not as fast as we wish they'd move, but still."

"That's a good thing, then. I'll see you...well, when I see you. You want to talk to your mom some more?"

"I wish, but I have to go. Thank you both."

Assured that everything was calm on the home front, Jordan went to back to work. While they were waiting for the location of Tim's cell phone to be identified, they needed to come up with a strategy regarding Salter.

✎

Jordan and Ellie were barely back at their respective desks when their cell phones rang at the same time. Ellie's showed an unknown number. She was immediately on alert when she realized who the caller was.

"I wanted to let you know right away. Well, James said I had to tell you right away."

There was no mistaking the utter relief in Michael's voice.

"You talked to him? That's great!"

"Yes. He told me to get you the notes you needed, since it's not information on any of his clients. In fact, he wants me to do it now."

"Hang on a second. Is Officer Martin nearby?"

"On the phone."

Jordan waved to indicate that she was speaking to Wes.

"Okay, I'll send someone over to get those notes. Thank you so much for calling. If you need anything, let us know, and give James my best."

"Thank you, Ellie."

"You're welcome. Talk to you later." She ended to call and directed her attention to Jordan who was still on the phone with Wes Martin, looking pensive.

"I understand. Thanks." She, too, laid the phone aside. "So, on the bright side, James is doing better, but he couldn't make an ID. This reminds me of something that happened in the Boyd case though. You suggested that it could be related to the Salter case," she said to Ann McCoy who nodded.

"Salter is straying from his Dad's MO," Bethany said. "Random violence...Maybe this wasn't so much about McKenzie's notes after all."

"It's possible, but how does that help us? We have a lot of theories, but the only person who could vaguely identify him was Annie Walton. If she's our best witness, it's still all going to fall apart."

"Or we find them alive, and they'll be able to tell their story," Bethany suggested, as if that wasn't obvious to everyone.

‹❦›

The man coming back to the room was a bad thing. Him not coming back at all, they had to learn, was a bad thing as well. Instead of being trapped with a monster, they were now simply trapped.

"We're going to die in here, aren't we? We're going to starve to death."

Tim felt an irrational resentment toward Owen who was just pointing out the obvious. They hadn't had a meal in, he wasn't sure how much time. Hours? A day?

He cast a look at the half-filled water bottle, the last thing the kidnapper had left with him. He wondered if Owen had one of those bottles within reach, too, and how much water was left in it. Those thoughts caused a pang of guilt, and he didn't even understand why.

They were the same.

Trapped. About to starve.

"No, we're not. The police are looking for us. Maybe they caught him."

"Then why aren't they here now?"

Oh, shut up, Tim wanted to say. He held back the words, because they were pointless. Perhaps it was Owen who had a point.

"My teacher's sister is with the police," he said. "They won't stop looking."

"Doesn't matter if they don't know where to look."

"Stop it. We can't give up now."

"No? I don't see why we should be so hopeful. We're going to hell, right? Maybe the people who said that were right. Maybe we're there already."

In fact, Tim's own parents had told him, but as long as they were alive, as long as there was a sip left in that damn bottle, he refused to believe it. Professor McCoy wasn't cursed. In fact, she was living in a nice house with her family. They seemed happy, leading more normal lives than a lot of straight people he knew.

There was still a small chance that he, or Owen, could have that too.

He sank back against the naked wall, the air in the room stuffy all of a sudden. Maybe it wasn't the water he had to worry about, but the amount of air?

Would there be anything left for them outside this place?

Chapter
Nineteen

E llie found Jordan in the break room, sitting on the bench, leaning forward with her head in her hands. She straightened at the sound of footsteps.

"Anything new?"

"Not really. Wes came with James's notes, but so far, it's nothing beyond what we expected. He claimed he was dating the girl, and that she had lied about her age. It was 'another time,'" she said, making quotation marks with her fingers. "His lawyer, the judge, the prosecutor, all white men who thought it wasn't fair to mess with his future too much, but he dropped out anyway."

"Another time, huh?" They both knew that there were still offenders that got away with the same tried and tired excuse. "We're not getting anywhere with Salter. He's not going to give up their location. He wants them to die."

"Not if we can get to the phone first."

"That's a big if at this point, and we haven't even started to talk about Ariel."

"Right," Ellie agreed. "We will when there's time. I think Becca already made her understand that this is serious. We don't want to scare them with the possibilities." In spite of the dire situation, she was glad it was Jordan who brought the subject up. "How are you doing?"

"I'm fine. I'm not the one who's locked up in some serial killer's hideout. I'm sorry. This is beyond frustrating."

"It is. Let's get more coffee, and we'll go from there?"

Jordan gave her a tired, but grateful smile.

"It's a start."

Carroll looked doubtful. "I'm not sure what you're hoping to achieve. You should all go home, take a few hours, come back tomorrow."

There was an air of frustration belying his words. He knew as well as they did that a few hours could make all the difference in the world to the missing men.

But Salter wasn't budging, and it seemed like they had no leverage left, nothing that he responded to.

"He thinks he's so clever and unique," Jordan said. "There's nothing new or unique about him. They all want to same thing."

She was aware of the looks on her. Only Ann McCoy's was curious. Everyone else in the room could easily make the connection, still.

"We tried every possible angle," Bethany said. "I'm sorry, but unless you can do magic, or something illegal, I don't see how we can proceed here."

"I hate to admit it, but I think she's right," Derek conceded, prompting a wry smile from Bethany.

"Let me try," Jordan insisted. "If it doesn't work, I'm ready to call it a night."

"All right, Carpenter." Carroll's quick turn left no doubt in anyone that he, too, was running out of options, all while Monday morning kept coming closer. "Remember, boundaries are a good thing."

She nodded, aware that he was more concerned about her guarding her own boundaries. Jordan wasn't sure how to feel about that fact, but she'd address it another day.

"Good. Let's do this."

Atwood had been replaced by an older officer. Salter sat in the chair, staring off into space when she entered the room. He flinched at the sound of the chair scraping on the floor. Not on purpose. She saw his nostrils flare at the scent of the coffee she'd brought with her.

On purpose.

"Something's up," he declared. "You're keeping me here all night because you realize you can't hold me forever?"

"Don't worry about that, Eric. You'll be charged with a multitude of crimes, including the murder of your father. That's not going to go away."

"Then why do you keep bothering me?"

Jordan took a sip of her coffee, then another, as if she was taking time to think about an answer. She noticed that he, too, looked tired.

"We have a problem here, right? We want something from you. You're not going to give it to us, I see that. So, I'm wondering what it is that *you* want from all of this."

"I don't know what you mean."

"I think you do. Look, I've met people who have killed, and most of the time, there's money involved, or revenge. That's not the case here, is it? You didn't go for the sons of rich families. Tim, or Owen, or Ashton, they didn't even know you."

She couldn't be too sure with him, but at least it seemed like he was paying close attention to her words.

"But you knew them. You stalked them. There was something that drew you to them."

You were my favorite. That line, and the tone of his voice, would stay with her forever. It also gave her a unique insight into the mind of someone like Salter, whether she appreciated it or not.

"But whatever you witnessed as a teenager, whatever you did, or your father, that's not enough if no one knows about it."

His eyes were wide, his face flushed.

"You wouldn't understand."

Even though it nearly made her face hurt, Jordan managed a smile. "See, that's where you are mistaken. One of the murderers I met…He wanted to kill me. To punish me. And he wanted to make sure we told the story correctly."

"Punish you for what?" It was hard to tell whether the emotion flickering over his face was excitement or alarm.

Jordan leaned back in her chair and drank from her paper cup. It might look like a comfortable stance to him, meanwhile the tension that had gripped her bordered on painful. She might be doing this for nothing.

"At the moment, the narrative is still all about your father, the power he had, the crimes he committed, yet he left us with nothing but dusty bones. You won't be able to get out of this, but you have the chance to claim the narrative, from him, like you always wanted."

"Punish you for what? I want to know."

She had a fleeting thought for the man who had founded a fan club for Darby, following her around with questions like that. This was on her, though. She had put herself in this situation—and she was in control of it.

"Deviant sexual behavior," she said, which was close enough to a working truth she needed in order to connect with Salter. "Come on, Eric, everyone's tired. There's always a story. If you don't tell yours now, someone else will do it for you. You don't want that, do you?"

"It's not that complicated," he said, casting a longing look at her coffee. "There are only two kinds of humans, predators, and prey."

"You were prey as long as your father was still alive."

"They put themselves out there. They needed me, to put them out of their misery." All of a sudden, he sat up straight. "Maybe you needed him too."

Jordan held his gaze unflinching, though his words crept past her guard, finding their mark. Not much longer now, and she would go home to her wife and daughter. Salter couldn't come back from this.

"Their parents didn't want them. The world didn't want them. At least for a while, they had purpose. I gave them purpose!" he yelled, then, lowering his voice again, he added, "There you have your answer. We give you purpose."

There might have been some truth to that, though not in the sense he meant it. Protecting society from the likes of him had always been a strong motivator. Seeing him walk into the trap did come with a sense of satisfaction.

Ellie was equally spell-bound and disturbed watching the interrogation. She had had her own considerable successes. She wasn't sure she'd be ready to tap that deep into her most traumatic experiences to get a suspect to talk, but it was working. She didn't appreciate the buzzing of her cell phone, but reading the message, she was convinced to call right back. Jill Allen was a reporter who had become a friend during recent cases, and she wouldn't write that kind of text if it wasn't urgent.

"We got scooped," she said without preamble. Ellie reluctantly stepped outside the room.

"Jill, I'm sorry, but I'm still at work…"

"This is about work, yours and mine. I wanted to let you know we'll be careful, but I can't promise the same about the competition. I saw another paper's headline that said *Police Department in Disarray*, and they're talking about increased incompetence, lack of leadership and budget cuts. I thought you might want to comment on that."

"Thanks for letting me know, but you'll have to take that to the communication department."

"I did. They, and your lieutenant said, no comment."

That struck her as strange. "There's going to be a press conference on Monday morning."

"People's patience is running out." Jill's tone was apologetic. "We keep seeing the parents on TV, and there doesn't seem to be any progress. That, and Noah Shriver resurfacing…"

"How did you—" Ellie broke off her sentence, aware that at this stage, she shouldn't give away anything, not even to Jill. "Look, let's talk tomorrow, okay? There's a lot going on right now, and I promise you, you will have answers eventually. I'll call you."

She went back into the observation area to watch Jordan going in for the kill, so to speak.

❧

For a few seconds, she felt like the floor had opened under her, and it wasn't for the nightmares she had knowingly invited. Salter using past tense when he talked about the victims couldn't mean anything good.

"That's better, right? You, telling your own story. I understand it now. Just tell us where we find the bodies."

170

Time was ticking by in tense silence. Jordan worried she might have gone too far, but then he leaned forward to whisper, "You're damn right it's my story. Daddy hadn't taken care of prey in a long time."

"Tell me where we need to go."

He did.

When her phone rang a second time, Ellie was tempted to turn it off altogether. Realizing the caller was Kate, currently at home with Meri, there was no chance. She realized Kate had tried to call before, while Ellie had still been on the phone with Jill. With a hammering heart, she accepted.

"Thank God," Kate said.

Ellie's stomach lurched.

"First of all, I want you to know, she's going to be fine. They told me it's just a little ear infection, and that was the reason for the fever, but they want to keep her overnight. I'm so sorry, Ellie, she wouldn't stop crying. I didn't know what to do, so I took her to the ER."

After taking a deep breath, and another, Ellie was able to sound fairly reassuring. "No, listen, that was a good thing."

Kate's nerves seemed frayed already. One of them needed to stay calm, though Ellie wasn't sure she could keep it up. Meanwhile, Jordan was in a room with a serial killer convincing him to give up the location of bodies, when they had hoped to find those victims alive.

Meri. In the ER. With an ear infection.

"I'll be right over. I just have to talk to Jordan."

"They assured me she'll be okay. I can stay here with her as long as you need me to. I don't mind skipping a class tomorrow."

While she appreciated all the reassurances, Ellie knew she wouldn't be okay until she saw Meri and talked to the doctor, and she knew the same was true for Jordan.

But could she tell her when they were about to leave for Salter's hideout? There was no way she couldn't tell her.

Hastening back to the observation area, she arrived at the same time Jordan stepped out of the room.

"I kind of want to take a shower now, but let's see this through first."

"I'll pretend you didn't completely ignore what I told you about boundaries," Carroll grumbled. "Good work."

Ellie briefly wondered what his strategy regarding the press was. She couldn't worry about that now. There was a somber atmosphere among her colleagues. They might be able to close the case, but they already had lost the race against time.

"Jordan," she said. "I need to talk to you. It can't wait."

"I'll be at the car," Derek said.

Detective McCoy went with Maria Doss.

"Tell me on the way," Jordan said, but halfway into Ellie's statement, she stopped in the middle of the hallway as if she couldn't believe what Ellie was saying.

Ellie didn't blame her. This night could hardly get more surreal.

Chapter Twenty

F or the longest time, Jordan had resented her biological
mother for choosing drugs and oblivion over her. This
wasn't the same thing. She had signed up to do this job, including all the rewards and the horrors that came with it. Families
and loved ones deserved closure, and so she was heading to a
crime scene while her baby was in the ER. Not alone. She knew
Kate to be kind and capable, a former cop about to be a lawyer,
Ellie's best friend. Ellie would be there soon. From the first day
of her life, Meri knew she was surrounded by loving adults.

It wasn't the same.

"I'm not sure how you did it," Derek admitted. "I don't think
anyone thought we'd do this tonight."

"We'll still be too late."

He didn't argue with that particular point. "Nothing that
happened tonight is about anything you did wrong, so don't go
there. Babies get bugs."

She couldn't help smiling at that. "I didn't know you were an
expert on babies."

"I'm not, but the doctors in that unit are, and if they say
Meri's going to be okay, she will be. They're doing their jobs,
and we have to do ours."

"Yeah," she said, leaning back into her seat. "I'm sure Detective McCoy wished for a different outcome."

"We all did. But he's never going to get out. You got him."

"Yeah. I guess I did." They were silent after that, steeling themselves for the sight that awaited them.

⁂

"You're going to be okay?"

The structure looked quite different from the hasty addition made to Charles Salter's house, though Jordan doubted that it was registered anywhere with the city. At first sight, it looked like a storm shelter, though they weren't in an area where those were a familiar sight.

Casting a look at those steps leading into pitch black darkness, she remembered the beginning of this case, the floor giving way under Sam who fell through the planks and broke her arm. She remembered another set of stairs leading down to a killing room—but this wasn't about her. Jordan realized she was relieved Ellie wasn't here, if not for the same reason.

They made it down to a lower level where they found something resembling a small kitchen and pantry. Dishes and canned goods on shelves, everything looked surprisingly clean.

"Is there anybody? Can you hear me? Please help!"

She spun around, the flashlight capturing Derek's stunned expression, she was sure, was mirroring her own. A male voice.

"We're the police," she shouted. "Where are you?"

"Behind some kind of wall," came the answer. "Please, hurry."

"We'll get you out of here," she promised. "What's your name?"

"I'm Tim Caplan," he said. "Owen is here, but he hasn't said anything in some time. I'm afraid he—"

"We'll get you out of here," Derek repeated Jordan's words while she looked around for something to break the wooden wall that separated them.

Tim Caplan was alive.

They'd come out of this night with one huge victory after all.

Owen Reed had been unconscious when they found him, but alive as well. Both men were taken to the hospital, and their parents were notified. Immediate medical care came first. Normally, Jordan would have been able to go home for a few hours, like the lieutenant had suggested what seemed like a lifetime ago.

Instead, she took a cab to the hospital, heading straight for the pediatric unit.

She found Ellie fast asleep in what looked like an uncomfortable position and gently woke her.

"Hey. They said we can take her home as soon as the paperwork is done. It's really all good. Fever's down, though I guess that's what made her cry earlier. I sent Kate away as well. I think we can take it from here."

They weren't doing so badly for people who had been up all night and been confronted with various high stress situations.

"We sure can," she said. "We found them alive, Ellie."

She hadn't expected Ellie to burst into tears, but Jordan wasn't that surprised either.

When Meri was asleep in her own bed, Jordan made a quick call to Lieutenant Carroll to inform him when she and Ellie would be coming in the next day. After a hot shower, they turned in for a few hours of sleep that were inevitably cut short by the alarm. A groan was all the reaction Ellie got from Jordan who pressed her face against the pillow.

"Come on. It's either that, or no breakfast, and I'm hungry."

"Okay. I'll go check on Meri."

She came to join Ellie in the kitchen a few minutes later, with Meri in her arms.

"She's still a bit fussy, but no fever."

"Thank God. You two just sit, I'm almost done here."

She finished preparing Meri's breakfast first, then poured coffee for Jordan and herself, and put two slices of bread in the toaster. They spent the next forty-five minutes focused on their shared meal.

Reality soon intruded when Pauline arrived to take over. Ellie related as much as she could of the past night's events to her.

"She should be fine," she said, kissing the top of Meri's head before she handed her to Pauline. "We'll be back home as soon as we can but call any time."

"Of course."

"Thank you," Jordan said. Her tone was wistful when she added, "See you later. We really appreciate you being here."

"You're welcome."

Neither of them wanted to leave, but they didn't have a choice.

⸻

At the hospital, the elation of having found both victims alive had given way to a more sober atmosphere. Both Caplan and Reed were treated for severe dehydration, and a number of injuries that told the stories of their ordeals.

Ann McCoy exited Tim's room when they arrived.

"Thank you for all your help," she said.

Ellie wondered how the situation with his parents, and Ann's sister, was going to work out. She hoped they'd be able to see past prejudice and to the fact that their son needed their unconditional support.

"It was great working with you," she said.

She nearly made a joke about how Ann could ask for a transfer, but then she remembered the conversation she'd had with Jill. That was no joke. She didn't even have the opportunity to talk to Jordan yet, as exhausted as they'd been when they returned home. Truth be told, she was still exhausted.

"You too." Ann sounded a tad wistful. "I'm glad they're alive, though they'll have a long way to go."

"When are you leaving?" Jordan asked. "You could come by for dinner if you like."

Ellie had a hard time hiding her surprise, with everything that was on their plate at this moment. Then again, it made sense.

The experiences of the past few days created a familiarity, much as being a woman in their profession did.

It seemed appropriate to mark the end of their cooperation.

Once again, she thought about Jill's remarks, wondering what these reports meant for the professional future of all of them.

That was a conversation for later.

⁂

"Okay, this is my suggestion." Bethany sounded sober. The task ahead was grueling for everyone involved. Mr. Reed—I'll go with you, Jordan. Ellie and Detective McCoy finish up Mr. Caplan's statement, so he doesn't have to go through this twice."

"Fine with me," McCoy said.

"Good. That leaves you with—" Bethany cast a look at Derek who nodded.

"Tying up loose ends with Salter. I got it."

"Then we're all set. Let's go."

"Sometimes she still forgets she's not the boss, but who can blame her when we all fall in line?" Derek whispered to Jordan.

"I thought you two made up."

"We did. I still notice."

"You have any better suggestions?"

"No, that's the thing. She's always right on top of it."

While she appreciated what he was trying to do, Jordan couldn't come up with much of a reaction. Bethany was right. They had to get this over with, for everyone who was a part of this.

"Good luck, anyway," she said.

"You too." They parted ways, and Jordan caught up with Bethany.

***

"Hi, Tim," Ann said softly. "We haven't met, but you know my sister Chrissie."

"Professor McCoy? Wow. I swear I told her everything when I knew it. I didn't mean to get her in trouble."

"She's not, and you don't have to worry about any of this. She was very relieved to hear the news. You'll be able to go home with your parents soon, after Detective Harding and I take your statement."

"We have to do this, right?"

Ellie noticed that his energy seemed to be waning quickly. They wouldn't have a big window. She wondered how Jordan was doing in the other room with Owen Reed, Ariel's friend. Perhaps Bethany's presence could be helpful in this context.

"I'm afraid so," she said. "We're just going to ask you a few questions. Answer them best you can."

"I'll try. Everything I can do so you'll put him away for good."

"Oh, we'll do that, there's no doubt about it."

"Your parents thought you ran away," Ann said. "What happened?"

His gaze clouded over. "I wanted to get away for a few days, clear my head. I meant to stay in touch with everyone, I just—"

"I know this is hard. Take your time."

Ellie felt overly aware of all the times she'd used the same line, wondering if they were any help at all. But they had to move forward.

"I was so mad at my parents...I was going to call a friend, but then I met this guy at a gas station, and he gave me a ride for a few miles. After that, a trucker picked me up. He didn't talk much, eventually dropped me off at a rest stop. I was starting to think, this could work out. Just have a time-out in a different place, clear my head. I walked from there to a train station. I had lunch in the restaurant, and I was trying to figure out what I'd do next."

"Did you talk to anyone?"

"No, but...I sat there for about half an hour. At some point, I got another coffee, later I went to the restroom and...Sorry, it gets blurry after that."

"That's normal. He used various drugs."

His eyes widened, the tension in his body unmistakable as he came to the darker place in his narration. "I remember feeling all detached when I woke up in that place, like...high," he said after a moment of hesitation. "It didn't feel real, like a nightmare."

Ellie exchanged a quick glance with Ann McCoy, wondering what demons of hers were wakened by Tim's story. She was certainly aware of her own. This also meant Tim couldn't have been with Salter at Rigley's. Someone lucky enough to get away?

"I was more lucid at some point, but I'm sorry if I'm not doing this right. It was all unreal, most of the time. I realized..." His eyes welled up, and he wiped his face in a quick angry gesture. "He freaking cooked for us. There was someone else in the other room, Ashton. I could hear him scream. After that...the silence, it really got to me, you know what I mean? It was so damn silent."

"Did the man ever talk to you?"

He laughed bitterly. "Did he talk? Guy wouldn't shut up. At first it was about him wanting to be friends. I was naïve enough to think I could talk him out of...the rest, but no. How stupid is that, thinking you can reason with someone once they chained you to a wall somewhere underground?"

"It's human," Ellie said. "You did what you had to in order to survive, and you made it."

"They won't tell me how Owen's doing. I was afraid he wasn't going to make it. I don't think I would have been able to stand that silence again."

"He's recovering, and he's getting the help he needs. So will you."

"My parents will think I brought this on myself somehow."

"Your parents will have to understand that nothing that happened to you was your choice or fault." Ann's voice was calm, though Ellie sensed her anger, for more than the trouble the Caplans had caused her sister. She understood perfectly why Jordan did what she did. The maddening reality they were dealing with made it even more important that they stayed in positions of authority. Their word meant a lot to someone like Tim. Budget cuts be damned.

"Yeah, good luck with that."

Ellie took a deep breath, bracing herself for the fact that this wouldn't be over as quickly as she'd hoped it would be.

Chapter
Twenty-One

J ordan had to admit that she'd never been that good at finding balance. But the results she'd produced always spoke for themselves. She pushed ahead, neglected her boundaries when she had the chance to get through to a ruthless murderer or a survivor reluctant to tell their story.

As a wife and mother, she wasn't responsible just for herself any longer. Jordan knew she would have to do better at finding that balance.

Owen Reed had agreed to talk to the police, though he was still under fairly heavy medication. Jordan noticed that both of his hands were bandaged.

Bethany introduced the two of them, and added, "I want you to know that we have access to your medical reports, so we don't have to go over every single detail."

He nodded. "I...don't remember much."

It was a good thing that they had Salter's description of his hideaway on tape. People like him liked to brag too damn much—all it took was to find the right angle. They loved explaining what they did, and why they did it, implying the rest of society was too scared and too dumb to follow the same impulses. They used drugs not to dull the pain but confuse their victims.

"That's okay. Let's start with what you remember."

Halfway through his stumbling, painful narrative, the ringing of Jordan's cell phone made him jump. She excused herself and stepped out of the room to answer to Anna Crawford, head of the lab.

"Can this wait? We're in the middle of something here."

"We found a ton of hidden files on Salter's laptop. You might want to see this."

Her stomach lurched in anticipation of what Anna was going to say next. "Want is a big word. I assume it's bad?"

"You're right. They are grouped by names and dates."

"Can you tell me if Oliver Boyd is one of them?"

"Nothing as bad as some of the others, but yes, there are some pictures that show he stalked him."

"I'll be right there," Jordan said and ended the call. Back in the room, she told Bethany, "I'm sorry, something urgent came up. Could you finish Mr. Reed's statement?"

"Jordan. Wait. Mr. Reed, I'll be back in a minute."

Bethany followed her outside. "What was that all about?"

Jordan leaned back against the wall. From here, she could see the clock on the other end of the hallway. It wasn't even noon yet.

"This will do him in for good. Our lab found a hidden video library on Salter's laptop."

To her surprise, Bethany looked indecisive.

"You go back in," Jordan told her. "They need someone there right away."

"This is going to be—"

"Horrible, I know. It will make sure he never gets out. I'm fine with that."

"All right. I'll meet you later at the station." She might have wanted to say something else, but Derek appeared at the same moment.

"See you there," he said.

On the way to the car, Jordan explained what Crawford had told her.

"You know, Maria is there as well. You don't have to do this."

"If we're starting to pick and choose with everything that might bring up bad stuff, there's not much left. Don't worry. I'll be fine."

"Okay. Dinner at your place tonight? We'll bring something. Kate still feels bad..."

"It wasn't her fault. She did the right thing," Jordan cut him off. "But yeah, you can come by if you don't stay too long."

Given what lay ahead of them, she couldn't bear to think of Meri right now. She needed to focus.

Ellie couldn't wait to go home. But as she watched her colleagues and friends still engaged in conversation, discussing the end of this far-reaching case, she knew she wouldn't be able to relax without clearing up something. She went to knock on Carroll's door, and he called her in.

"Sir. I was wondering if I could talk to you for a moment."

"As long as it only takes a moment, sure. Sit."

She did, perching on the edge of the seat. Appropriate. Maybe.

"What's the matter?"

There was no turning back now.

"Earlier, I received a call from a journalist—" She noticed the change in his expression and hastened to add, "I trust her, but she said other papers will come out with a story about the department before Monday."

"I'm sure you meant to ask a question."

She did, indeed. Ellie hadn't had much time to obsess about what Jill had told her, and what it meant for everyone's careers, if anything. She couldn't ignore that she'd been the last detective to join the unit. If any cuts were made, she might have reason to worry.

"I didn't tell her anything because I don't know anything. If those budget cuts come through, is my job still safe?"

"Somebody jumped the gun here. We're not talking about letting anyone go at this point."

"It won't be just one newspaper."

His answer wasn't much of a consolation to Ellie.

"I'm aware, and we'll take care of that." He seemed to sense that she wasn't satisfied and continued. "This is a subject that comes up on a regular basis. You caught Salter, and you found two of his victims alive. That's what they should be writing about. You're doing good work, and so is everyone else here. If anyone needs a reminder, I'll be happy to give it. If anything, we should hire. I looked into hiring Shriver at some point, but obviously that was a long time ago."

"Really? He claimed that he was never given a shot."

"He's been claiming a lot of things. Where are we on that, by the way?"

"His face is out there. Nothing yet from the hotline, but everyone's on alert." All of a sudden, she was worried that it might not be enough, for various reasons.

"Make sure you put a stop to this. That's another headline we don't need."

Imcompetence. Disarray. Ellie had to agree. Shriver's story would only add fuel to the fire.

"I'll check with everyone before we go home."

"You do that."

He, too, looked exhausted. When Ellie left the office, she realized she wasn't feeling reassured at all, and whatever changes were coming, could impact more than her job.

⁂

The videos dated back seven years, overlapping with some cases they had suspected Charles Salter in. This was far from the quick wrap-up they had imagined, and it was later than anyone had envisioned when they finally took down the wall.

"You had the right instincts about Boyd all along," Derek told her as they were placing photographs back into their respective files.

It was cold comfort. Her first case after she'd been back to work had made her doubt her skills for some time. But Salter had beaten up Jerry, a man Oliver Boyd met the same night, and he had followed Oliver to the campground.

"McCoy, too, thought that there was a connection. Eric didn't always plan as carefully as his father," she said. "Sometimes, it was just about the violence."

"McKenzie."

"Yes. I should check on him soon."

"This is...a lot, but at least we could make all those connections now. This is over."

"Thank God it is."

The images would haunt her for some time to come, but he was right. They had done right by the victims, and the city was safer for it.

"I guess tomorrow will be all about the paperwork."

"Monday will be okay." The lieutenant had joined them, casting a pensive look at the files and piles of paper and photographs. "Carpenter, I talked to Dr. Roberts. I want you both at the press conference Monday morning."

"Understood."

"It's important that we put faces to the work we do here," he said. "You all get some rest. I'll see you on Monday."

"Was that strange?" Jordan asked when he had left the room.

"A little," Derek confessed. "I don't blame him. He has a lot of politics to consider."

"That didn't sound like business as usual."

"I guess we'll find out on Monday. I can't believe I'm saying this, but I'm ready for dinner. I'll call Kate."

"I'm going to find Ellie and McCoy. See you at home?"

"You will."

She thought he was going to say more, but he simply patted her shoulder and left. Fortunately, not everything needed to be put in words. She, too, was glad to be back after all the detours and obstacles.

⌾

Ellie had planned to take a moment to talk to Jordan about what she'd learned from the lieutenant, but now that they had guests over, she decided to wait until later. Whatever happened might affect all of them in same way, save for McCoy, and she wanted to have that conversation with Jordan first.

They had invited Jack and Pauline to stay as well. For once, she and Jordan had been able to put Meri to bed, something she was grateful for after this day. Afterwards, everyone sat down for dinner provided by the *SEVEN*. As promised, Derek and Kate had paid, and they'd brought enough to have plenty of leftovers.

Those videos. The images lingered on her mind.

She would never get used to what some people were willing to do to others out of hate. Those images seemed surreal in the safety of their home where they were surrounded by friends and family. She hoped that the victims' families would find it in their hearts to see past their prejudice.

"I had conversations with folks back home. The good news is that the Caplans changed their mind on the gay conversion BS," Ann McCoy said. "For how long, I'm not sure, but it gives Tim a time-out at least. The bad news is that they still want to get my sister fired."

"No court will side with them," Derek said.

"Sadly, I wouldn't be so sure these days, but if the employer is reasonable, I assume it won't go that far."

"They seem to be decent," Ann said. "But damn it. Even if this wasn't personal, I can't believe parents behaving like this, no matter how often I see it. I wish there was more of a way to hold them accountable, at the very least, for making our job harder."

"Amen," Jordan said, clinking her bottle against Ann's. "See? That right there makes sense. You know, I think the department might be hiring soon. How about it?"

"I wish," Ann said wistfully. "But I have a lot to take care of at home."

"We get that. We really do." Ellie cast a look at the food still on the table. "We should put this away. Jordan? Could you give me a hand?"

"Sure." Jordan got up and picked up a couple of bowls. She followed Ellie who carried a plate and the breadbasket back to the kitchen.

"Don't worry, I wasn't serious, and she didn't think I was—though I think she'd fit in with us."

"Yeah, about that."

"You're not worried because I had a couple of beers? It's Sunday tomorrow."

"Jordan. You might not want to promise a job to anyone."
Ellie sighed. Jordan, understanding that they were long past
jokes, cast her a concerned glance.

"What's going on?"

"Jill called me...that seems like forever ago new. Yesterday.
There's going to be a story out tomorrow, about inefficiency
and coming cuts to the department."

"Wow. Okay. Nice of her to warn us. That's why you were
talking to Carroll earlier?"

"It's not Jill's story, someone got ahead of them. And yes, I
was talking to him. He said not to worry, but it didn't sound
very convincing to me."

"So that's why he wants me at the press conference. He knows
a shake-up is coming."

"I'm not sure I'd call it that, but Jordan, if they start to let
people go, I'll be the first."

Ellie hadn't known how scary that notion was until she said
it out loud.

"We're not there yet, not by a long shot."

"But you think it's possible? I can't imagine where this is
going. I had this one other interview. We're already on a tight
schedule day to day, and if I had a long commute, I'd be—"

"Ellie. Stop." Jordan laid her hands on her shoulders, interrupting the flow of words. "If the worst-case scenario happens,
you might be reassigned, not let go. They have no reason what-
soever. And this is Homicide. They're not going to mess with
us."

"I hope you're right."

"Carroll will do the press conference, and that will change the
press coverage. We'll have to do a mountain of paperwork, and
everything will be back to normal."

"Except Shriver is still out there."

"Yeah." Jordan sighed. "I really don't want to think about this now."

Ellie could sympathize though she was afraid they would have to return to the subject soon enough.

Chapter
Twenty-Two

A nn was the first to call it a night.

"Thanks again for all your help—and dinner." She took out her phone to call a cab.

"We should go too," Jack announced. "We could drop you off at your hotel."

"That would be great. Thank you."

"It's no problem."

After a round of goodbyes, Ellie, Jordan, Derek and Kate had one last drink.

Despite her earlier warnings, Jordan had decided with Ellie that they weren't going to wait to bring up the subject. It didn't affect Ann, and they didn't want to worry Jordan's parents. Everyone else, maybe, had a reason to worry, or perhaps they just needed a bit of mutual reassurance.

"No way," Derek said. "They can't fire either of us. We still have the best closure rate in the department. It's a record. And we're Homicide—no one's cutting Ellie's job either."

"That's what I told Ellie. With Waters gone, and Shriver definitely not getting his spot, I don't see whose job they could cut."

It was perhaps the sum of it all, the pressure of the past few days crashing down on her, but Jordan couldn't help wondering if her interaction with Mayfield's mother played a role. She had apologized, and to her knowledge, there had been no further contact between the department and the Mayfields' lawyer.

A part of her remained wary.

"It wouldn't make sense," she agreed. Bureaucracy didn't always make sense. But they had just put Salter away for good and found Reed and Caplan alive. That had to count for something.

"I'm sure it will be fine," Kate said. "And I'm so happy Meri is okay. I'm sorry for scaring you."

Apparently, they weren't the only ones needing reassurance. Jordan still felt like her heart skipped a beat when she thought of the moment Ellie had told her.

"You handled it the best way anyone could have."

"Maybe, but that really got me thinking. I love Meri, and I'll be happy to babysit her whenever I have time, but wow, I can't imagine doing that as a full-time job. I'd freak out so much."

"That's not true. You'd be great," Derek insisted.

A somewhat awkward silence followed his words. Kate shook her head. "No offense, but I'm glad we didn't make any plans. I do, however, have to study tomorrow, and I think you two need some time too. How about we call it a night?"

No one argued with her.

When she and Ellie returned to the living room and picked up glasses to carry into the kitchen, Jordan asked, "Did you catch that?"

"Between the lines, but yeah, I did. They'll figure it out. Kate was always pretty adamant about not wanting kids."

"She changed her mind on other things," Jordan reminded her.

"Yeah, but that's not really any of our business. How about we take care of these tomorrow?" she said with regard to the dishes.

"I love that idea."

Before she went upstairs for the bedroom, Ellie tugged on her hand and pulled her close. "I love you," she whispered. "Today was...rough."

"Yes, it was. But we're here. Meri will be fine. It's a win."

"You were amazing."

For Jordan, today's achievements were nothing but a return to something that felt fairly normal. It was a precarious victory. She was still coming to terms with the fact that it wasn't the exact same place she'd been before. Experiences had changed the trajectory.

"I'm glad you think so. Let's get some sleep."

⌘

It was around five a.m. when they tiptoed into Meri's room assuring themselves that their daughter was still sleeping soundly. Back in the bedroom, Ellie thought about the articles that would come out today, and the upcoming press conference. Even if they'd been successful regarding the father and son serial killer duo, the press would still have questions about Shriver.

They'd spent a big chunk of Monday putting the horrors Salter's victims had experienced, into words.

But they had a moment of peace left before it all began.

Back in bed, she didn't pull the covers up, but leaned in to kiss Jordan, finding herself in the warmth of her embrace a moment later.

193

"I was hoping you'd have the same idea," Jordan murmured, her hand brushing over Ellie's hair and then her back, fingertips following the line of her spine. She was wide awake in a heartbeat, her body thrumming with the expectation of pleasures to come.

"You know me. It's pretty much always on my mind, but it's getting harder to make time."

"No kidding. But we have time now."

Ellie bit her lip when Jordan's hand slid past the waistband of her panties. They were going to make the most of that time.

They enjoyed a fairly leisurely breakfast as a family, the first in a while with just the three of them. Neither Ellie nor Jordan were in a hurry to get to their phones. If the lieutenant thought it was okay to take a day, a Sunday nonetheless, it was what they'd do.

"I wasn't just talking about that earlier, when I said amazing."

Jordan smiled as she refilled their coffee cups. "Be honest, you meant that, too."

"Sure, I won't deny it. But it reminded me when I first watched you in an interrogation. I wanted to be you."

"Then at some point, you realized all the baggage that came with that, and you realized it's better to be Ellie Harding."

"You are so wrong. I admire you even more, knowing all you've dealt with."

"I didn't make it easy on anyone. I'm sorry. This, finally, it feels different. I was so afraid I'd be going backwards, but I think I made it past that."

"You did."

"I remember when you looked at me that way."

"I never stopped," Ellie said and suppressed a curse the next moment when her cell phone started vibrating. "It's Jill. Perhaps I should take it."

"Go ahead. Sadly, we can't hide out here forever."

Meri clapped her hands, and they couldn't help laughing.

"I'm glad you're happy, though I'm not sure that occasion warrants it," Ellie said dryly. "Yes, Jill. You're aware it's Sunday?"

"Do you have anything for me?"

"I told you the last time, sorry, but no. We've been a little busy, but if you must know? Off the record, my lieutenant told me we don't have to worry."

"I'm sure he's not lying to you, but I hear rumors about districts being redrawn, and precincts being merged. In fact, one of the papers is reporting about it today."

"Come on, Jill, you know we have a double shift behind us, and a baby at home. We'll be back at work tomorrow."

"I'll see you at the press conference, in any case."

"I'm sorry, Jill. There's nothing new I can tell you. We'll talk later?" Ellie ended the call and laid the phone back on the table. "Yeah, I didn't have to snap at her, but this is making me nervous."

"They don't know anything. Redistricting is a political thing. They want to see who's inefficient, that's not us."

Ellie leaned back in her seat and picked up her cup.

"I want to believe that, but it would really help if we caught Shriver. How could he stay hidden for so long? Let me rephrase that. How the hell did he survive that jump?"

❦

He tuned into the press conference when a stern-looking lieutenant was trying to make his case. In his opinion, Carroll deserved every bit of trouble that was coming his way, but that was not the reason to watch.

He studied her, as she was waiting her turn, and touched her face on the TV screen. The flash of exasperation in her expression made him smile. No doubt it was a reaction to her cell phone vibrating in the pocket of her pants. He couldn't see her reach for it to turn it off, but it was easy to deduce that was what happened.

He'd catch her another time.

He was patient, after all, and that conversation had been a long time coming.

Chapter
Twenty-Three

A couple of days later, Bethany came by to say goodbye before heading for the airport.

"I hope this works out for all of you. Well, if it doesn't, I'm pretty sure Taylor still wants you. Just say the word, and I'll make a phone call."

"Thanks, but that won't be necessary," Jordan told her. They had come a long way, she reflected. Back when they were in their relationship, it had often seemed like Bethany was trying to control every aspect of her life. Now, she was down to friendly meddling. But Jordan didn't need or want another job, no matter how attractive this position was. Taylor Hudson, a former colleague of both of them, was heading a new unit investigating links between domestic violence and terrorism. The last time Bethany had come to her with the offer, Jordan was about to give birth.

"I tell her I keep trying." Bethany shrugged. "I'm sure I'll see you all soon. Take care."

"You too."

After she left, they returned to their paperwork. Ellie was pouring over traffic camera footage and calls from the hotline while Jordan finished up her report.

She didn't think the lieutenant had sounded worried. Determined, for sure. Sober, after all the revelations about Salter and his father.

No, she couldn't imagine starting over in another city when she'd just laid down roots, with her family, in a new home.

After work, they stopped for a quick dinner at the *SEVEN*, where the TV showed a special coverage about *The Serial Killers Among Us.* Tim Caplan's parents thanked the local police department for finding their son.

While this was a relief after Sunday's news cycle, Jordan wondered if their emphasis on local was on purpose. Back at home, Ann McCoy had investigated Caplan's disappearance—the sister of the woman they were trying to get fired.

She winced when the report cut to the press conference, and she saw herself on the screen, frowning at no one in particular.

"Do you mind turning this off?" she asked Jack who complied after regarding the TV for a few seconds.

"You look tired," he commented. "I hope you can all take some time off after this?"

"No rest for the wicked," she said with a shrug. "I've taken a lot of time off in the past year."

"And for good reasons. The city should know what your work is worth."

"It will be okay," she said. "Could you check on our food? Thank you. We want to get Meri to bed as soon as possible."

"I'll be right back," he promised.

"Thank you."

"I thought you looked badass," Ellie commented. "Like, try to mess with me and find out what happens."

"Can I sit with you for a bit, or am I interrupting something?" Maria Doss joked.

"Funny. What else do you have?"

Maria set her bottle on the table and took a seat in one of the chairs. "Worries. I know Carroll has been low-key about it all, but the talk doesn't stop. Atwood is telling everyone who wants to know, and some who don't, that the, I quote, 'diversity hires' are first. Of course he mentions my name."

"Of course he does." Ellie made a frustrated sound. "He's one to talk about other people's qualifications. Why does he still have a job anyway?"

"Good question. The family lawyer's got it covered, I think." Maria sighed and got up again. "You two have a good night. I'll go check on Val...see what she thinks of me becoming a kept woman."

"Not going to happen."

"You never know."

❧

They were none the wiser regarding any possible changes in the department, or Shriver's whereabouts, when Ariel called the next morning.

"Hey. I was wondering if you or Jordan could drive me to my training camp on Saturday? Becca would do it, but I kind of wanted to talk to you."

"No problem," Ellie assured her. "We can come pick you up for breakfast. That way we'll have some time to talk, and one of us will drive you to the camp later."

"That would be great." Ariel sounded relieved. Ellie wondered if she had spoken to Owen Reed. Both of them had survived trauma, substantial in length and the amount of violence they'd been exposed to. They'd have to be careful, with each other and one's own boundaries.

"We'll see you Saturday morning, then."

Things were good.

Meri was back to her usual sunny disposition.

Atwood was the only one still talking about job cuts, and the headlines regarding the department had changed to more favorable ones.

Slowly, routine returned to their lives, even if it looked different from before.

Over breakfast that Saturday, Ariel shared that she'd seen Owen. She'd been able to talk to him alone.

"How did that go?" Jordan asked softly.

"Okay, I guess." She shrugged. "He doesn't blame me."

"Sweetie, why would he blame you? You came to us right away when you realized something was wrong."

Owen's phone had been found in one of the boxes in the underground hideaway.

"Yes, but perhaps I should have noticed sooner? I don't know. It's been a weird few days."

"No kidding." Jordan exchanged a look with Ellie, thinking that at least all her concerns hadn't cost Ariel her appetite. "You noticed. That's all that counts."

"Is it, really? I feel so stupid for thinking that I could trick this person into...something, maybe revealing where he held Owen. I could have done something right."

"Stupid, no way, though that could have been dangerous. You did the right thing. Ariel, from the moment we met you, you always did a whole lot more than your share. Nothing you did interfered with finding Owen."

"It didn't help much either. I'm really sorry."

"You have nothing to be sorry about," Jordan insisted. She cast a glance at her watch. "We can talk about this some more if you like, but I'm afraid you two will have to leave soon."

They had decided that Jordan would stay home with Meri while Ellie drove Ariel to the camp, a forty-five-minute drive out of town.

"Yeah, let's go."

Ariel leaned down to say goodbye to Meri, and Ellie used the moment for a quick, coded whisper. "Perhaps we could take a nap later?"

The smile playing over Jordan's lips told her she understood the message.

"I'd love to."

⁂

Ariel seemed less worried when they drove up to the camp, if still a little pensive.

"You know, Jordan told me about the book. I think it's a great idea that you focus on school and sports right now. You're doing really well."

"It's okay, yes."

"Is there anything else?" Ellie wasn't sure if it was the right moment to address that question, but it pained her to see Ariel doubt herself. She knew that Jordan had a hard time with it as well.

"No. It's just that it's been scary. With Owen, and be-fore...what happened to Jordan."

Ellie remained silent, aware that it was important to let Ariel talk.

"Back with the Prophets, Mom told me about the life out-side, and I often dreamed about it. I guess I thought that once we..." She swallowed hard. "Once I made it there, everything else would be easy. Or that there would be nothing else that scared me, because what could be worse than that? I still believed it, even after they told me that Mom was dead. Silly, right?"

"I don't know. I think we all do that, assume that once we just get over that one hurdle, everything will be fine."

"We have to adjust expectations?" Ariel asked, her tone and smile far too adult for her age. "I shouldn't complain. I know some really cool people, and you've all helped me. It's just been...a lot."

"You're right about that. And it's good to talk it through, but this weekend, you're going to kick some ass on the track...What's funny?"

"I imagine the look on their faces if a woman spoke like that...But they're in prison now, and we can say whatever we want, right?"

"Within reason," Ellie reminded her, but she had to laugh too.

Kathryn called to ask if Jordan and Ellie wanted to come to dinner the next week. Jordan talked to her while watching Meri who was playing on a blanket on the floor. After ending the call, she sat back, allowing herself a moment of gratitude for how things had played out.

She had struggled and stumbled after the attack, but she had made it back. She had a life and a family. She still had her career. Even the sharp edges of her childhood memories had softened. It didn't mean that she would ever forget about the severity of the situation. She was living her life in the present.

She couldn't wait for Ellie to get home and for once, have a quiet weekend. Amused, Jordan thought she could even do with not seeing their friends for a couple of days. They needed that time for themselves. It would start the moment Ellie returned which would be in an hour, at the latest.

Jordan sat down on the blanket with Meri, laughing when her cell phone rang, and Meri reached for it.

"Oh no, please give me another decade or so?"

She kissed her cheek before she picked up the phone and answered.

"Hello?"

"Hello, Jordan. I've missed hearing your voice."

Even though it had been a while, she recognized his right away, and she certainly hadn't missed him. Slowly, Jordan got to her feet, wondering how to best handle this.

"I heard you weren't dead."

"Don't disappoint me, please," Noah Shriver said. "I won't stay on long enough for the time it takes to notify your colleagues and try to trace this phone."

"Then what do you want? Wouldn't it be smarter to skip town?"

"You got the package?"

"You really don't need to send me things. Why don't we talk about this in person? You must be tired. If you turn yourself in..."

"I'll be charged with two counts of murder. No, thank you. But don't worry, we will talk."

"I hope you're not trying to threaten me."

"Come on. I've always liked you. You were the only one who listened to me. It's not you I have a problem with. I'll call you later."

He ended the call before she could react.

"There goes our weekend, baby," she told her daughter. "Damn him."

Chapter
Twenty-Four

"Are you sure this is the right way?" Ellie asked doubtfully when the directions Ariel provided led them to a road going up into the woods.

"You're a cop!" Ariel said, her voice colored with disbelief. "You were a patrol officer once, so you must know?"

"I've been around here before, but I'm not aware of any training camp in the vicinity. Sorry about that. Let me check the GPS."

"There's a gas station over there. Maybe you could ask?"

"I'm going to find it, don't worry. Let me just go get a bottle of water." Fortunately, the gas station had a small store attached. "We still have time."

"Sure."

"Do you want anything, a snack?"

"No, thanks." Ariel leaned back in her seat, smiling to herself. "But do ask for directions."

"You're quite the comedian this morning," Ellie told her.

Shriver kept his promise, even though he likely knew that the second time, he had an even smaller window. Jordan had dropped Meri off at her parents' and driven straight to the station.

"Hello, Noah."

"Sounds a little busy in the background. I was hoping for some more privacy."

"I'm sorry I can't do that right now. But we can talk about anything you want." She leaned back in her seat, rolling her eyes. "I'm here for you."

Derek and Maria were both present.

"You're still there?"

"You want to talk? Let's talk about how Daniels was going to fire me, and how none of your colleagues ever took me seriously. I'm tired of not being taken seriously."

"I understand. I know how that feels."

Yes, sure, I understand, she scoffed in her mind. He got entangled with a sex worker and a pimp, paid a substantial sum in a blackmail scheme before he killed them both.

"I know you do. Your wife didn't get it."

"Ellie has nothing to do with that," her response was swift and a tad too sharp maybe. Ellie had first connected the cases and interrogated Shriver. Of course he remembered that.

She had to keep him talking. Shriver wasn't a psychopath like Eric Salter, and she had gotten through to him.

"Oh, I don't know about that. She could have left it alone. I would still have a career."

He said that Lieutenant Daniels was about to fire him, just a few seconds ago. Of course it was always a woman that had failed him, his ex-wife, the sex-worker, the lieutenant, and the cop who put the pieces together.

"She was just doing her job, like all of us. That's all you ever wanted, right? Do the job. If you care about that at all, you'll take responsibility."

"Maybe I should have a word with her?" he surmised. A moment later, the line was dead.

Jordan muttered an expletive as she got to her feet. She wasn't going to leave anything to chance.

⁓

Ariel picked up her cell phone, sighing when she realized the battery was dead. She'd forgotten to charge it, too eager and anxious to have that conversation with Jordan and Ellie. Every time something went catastrophically wrong, Joy Anne attacking Jordan, Owen's kidnapping—it baffled her that people around her didn't think she was responsible.

Because she felt responsible all the time, like she had when she and her mom were living with the Prophets, and Ariel strived to protect her, and to protect younger girls. Somehow, she always seemed to fall short.

Ellie seemed to be taking a lot of time for a simple question and a bottle of water. Ariel exited the car and walked across the parking lot to the store, freezing in mid-motion. What she saw felt unreal. The young woman behind the counter, holding up her hands.

A man with a gun standing in front of her.

Ariel had been around more guns before than she cared to remember, and those had not been in the hands of good people. For a few painful seconds, she had the urge to go back to the car and hide on the floor of the backseat, memories rushing in threatening to overwhelm her. The day Agent Strickland was supposed to get them out, but her mom never made it. The moment she heard about what Joy Anne had done. Owen.

207

She couldn't freeze. She couldn't do nothing, again, but she didn't know what to do. There was no way she could drive the car to get help. Her cell phone was dead. She didn't even know if Ellie was okay...

Ariel straightened. Ellie knew how to take care of herself, but she'd need backup. There was one thing Ariel had going for her, the very reason for why she was going to the camp.

She had no more time to lose.

                      ❧

Ellie's biggest worry had been for Ariel waiting outside in the car. Once she'd assessed the situation to realize that the man in his mid-twenties was by himself, she silently approached him from behind with her weapon drawn.

"Drop the gun!" she yelled. "On your knees."

The young woman minding the store dove under the counter. To Ellie's relief, the man complied, and she kicked the gun away from him. Okay. This was going well enough, even if Ariel might be late to camp.

If she called in back-up now, perhaps her colleagues could take care of him, and she'd be back after driving Ariel. She'd have to call Jordan to make sure she didn't worry...all of those thoughts passed through her mind as she clicked the numbers, waiting for dispatch to come on.

"This is Detective Ellie Harding."

She didn't get further than that before a gunshot rang out. The man's body jerked once, and then he lay still—his own gun still a few feet away from him. Ellie's mind struggled to put the pieces together. It happened quickly when she heard a voice behind her.

"No need to make that call. I got your back, Ellie."

"Have you lost your freaking mind?" She took a deep breath, trying to calm herself. She couldn't talk to him like this, not with Ariel out there in the car, and the employee still cowering behind the counter. Ellie had turned off her phone as Shriver had instructed.

"I had it covered."

"This time, sure. But he'd get out in a few months, pull the same shit, perhaps get someone killed that time. Our job is about preventing crime, isn't that right?"

Perhaps it was smarter not to remind him that her job wasn't his any longer.

"You're right," she said, keeping her tone level. "You're absolutely right about that."

"Ma'am, you can come out now. It's safe. We got that son of a bitch, pardon my language."

Ellie heard crying from behind the counter. She didn't blame the woman. Nothing about this situation felt remotely safe.

"Get up now!" There was an edge to his tone that she didn't like.

"I know you don't want the police in here right now, but why don't we let her go?"

"Come on, Ellie. We are the police. But you're right, we don't need her. Ma'am? Your phone, please."

Reluctantly, the woman got to her feet. She was trembling. "I don't have one."

He fired another shot at the phone on the counter, plastic shards flying everywhere.

"Your phone," he said with a cordial smile. With shaking hands, she picked up her purse and emptied it on the counter.

Shriver took her phone. "I'm afraid my colleague and I have to leave, but first, please, get in there."

With the gun in his right hand, he indicated the door behind the woman, with the word *Private* on it. She looked hesitant. "You'll be fine. I'm not a monster, even though you might think that. Right, Ellie?" He hadn't let either one of them out of his sight or let them get close enough to try anything. He didn't seem to expect an answer from her either. "Come on, we don't have all day."

His tone had changed, his finger on the trigger tightening. The woman hurried to oblige. "One more thing. Keys."

This time, the employee handed them over without missing a beat, and Shriver locked the door behind her.

"That's it, we're ready."

"I'm not going with you."

"You don't want me to shoot her too, right? Then I believe you will."

<hr>

"Son of a—" Jordan stopped herself from finishing the expletive. She had the feeling Ellie would call her out on it. There were three cars in the parking lot. That of the man who had tried to rob the store, the employee's, and one she assumed to be left behind by Shriver.

He had taken Ellie's, to make sure he did what he could to piss her off.

Inside the store, the dead body was the first indication that things had gone horribly wrong in here. Ariel had only witnessed part of the drama before she took off running and didn't stop until she reached the camp, from where she had called 911.

Jordan crouched beside the robber's body, checking for a pulse though she wasn't surprised to find none.

"Is there anybody? Hello? Please help, I'm in here!" The employee. "He took the keys." The tearful voice sounded almost apologetic.

"This is Detective Carpenter. Don't worry. We'll have you out of there in no time."

That might have been an exaggeration, but Jordan needed some reassurance just as much as the woman on the other side of that door. She needed her statement now.

"What's your name?"

"Sandy. Sandy Reilly."

Fortunately, it didn't look very sturdy, so they might get it done without any tools.

"Okay, Sandy, could you please step away from the door?"

"Yes."

A well-placed kick was a good way to channel her frustration. The door sprang open, revealing the frightened employee cowering next to a shelf.

"Oh God, I hate my life so much right now, you know?" Sandy Reilly was near hysterical as she struggled to her feet. While Jordan couldn't blame her, she also had little patience for her or anyone at this moment. On the bright side, she didn't show any signs of physical harm.

"We have an ambulance on the way," Jordan assured her. "Are you hurt?"

"No. It's just that the store was held up twice in three months," Sandy continued. "I don't know what the hell they're thinking, maybe because it's remote, but you sure don't get rich from that."

"Can you tell me what happened next?" As they were talking, the store started to fill up with law enforcement personnel. Jordan was relieved to see that someone had covered the body, though Sandy Reilly didn't pay much attention to her surroundings as she spoke.

"The lady drew her gun on him, and he dropped his. I was so relieved when I realized she was a cop, right there at the right moment. I hid behind the counter to be out of the way, that's when I heard the gunshot. This other guy...He just shot him. I know it wasn't the woman, because she yelled at him."

"It's important. Did he say anything about where they were going to go?"

"No, he made me get in here and locked the door. He's not a real cop, is he?"

"Could you look at these pictures for a second, please?"

"Oh yes, that's her. And him. Jesus, and I thought it couldn't get worse after that punk pulled a gun on me."

That "punk" was now dead, and Sandy's description of the events fit Noah Shriver's entitled M.O. perfectly. Jordan found some comfort in knowing that his goal had always been to go after criminals. He also had an irrational view of who had supposedly done him wrong.

"Thank you, Sandy. I see the ambulance is here. Let's get you checked out, okay?" The medical examiner and her team were blocking Sandy's view on the way. They stepped outside, and Jordan handed her off to the paramedics. She turned to head back to the store, wincing at the pouring rain.

Think.

They had been on the way the moment Ariel made it to the camp and called them. She'd left while the robbery was still in progress, before Ellie intervened, and before Shriver killed the man.

"They can't have gotten that far," she said to Derek who regarded the scene with a frown. "He left the car."

"You think they're out there on foot?"

"It's the kind of thing he'd do," she said with disgust. "Anything to prove how tough and righteous he is, right?"

"Roadblocks are in place."

"That's not enough. We can't let him slip away one more time."

Chapter
Twenty-Five

Ellie knew that Shriver lived in his own version of reality. She didn't think that it was his goal to kill her, but she wasn't going to take chances either. He was smart, keeping her at a distance when he made her get into the car—her own—and then, after they'd parked near a dirt road. He kept a cordial tone when asking her to leave gun and phone in a ditch outside but fired a quick shot close to her feet when she didn't comply right away.

How did that quiet weekend turn into a hike in the rain with a cop turned felon who had lost it?

Her clothes were soaked. It had been warm and humid when she and Ariel had left in the morning, now the rain was coming down in sheets.

"I hope you have a plan here, and that it wasn't just both of us dying of pneumonia."

"I needed to talk to Jordan. Obviously, that's not going to happen, so we'll have to work with this."

Ellie walked in front of him, well aware of the gun pointed at her.

"You could have gotten away. Anywhere. You still could. There's nothing keeping you here. She's married," she said, holding her breath.

"Married people do change their minds. My ex did."

"I'm sorry about that. You deserved better. Sometimes, life is unfair."

"It is," he agreed. "Keep walking."

"Where are we going?" Ellie asked, but she complied.

"Somewhere quiet. Where we can finally have that conversation," Shriver said morosely. "You know it wasn't just about life being unfair. People sabotaged me. Your lieutenant. Daniels."

"I thought you liked working for her, but...All right, we'll talk."

"You sabotaged me, too."

"I didn't mean to. I'm really sorry." Hands still up, she stopped and turned around. He had holstered his gun.

"I wish things could have gone differently," Ellie went on, keeping her voice soft. "You've had a lot of bad breaks. Instead of running, if you sat down and told your story, all of it..."

She held his gaze for a few seconds, and then took her chance, finding herself on her back on the muddy ground the next moment, rocks digging into her back.

"Don't try," he warned, pointing the gun on her though he reached out a hand to help her up.

"I can do it."

"Don't be so fucking proud," he scoffed.

"Let her go!"

Jordan stood only a few feet away with her weapon trained on Shriver, cast in the unreal light of the lightning against the backdrop of the trees. Shriver started laughing though his voice was drowned out by the thunder.

"Yes, let's do it," he shouted. "Let's end it here, like this. Makes sense you'll be the one to do it."

He spun around, but Jordan was faster as she fired the shot. He dropped his gun, clutching his shoulder while Ellie reached for it before he could.

"Are you okay?"

"A bit banged up. And wet. Otherwise, yes."

Jordan crouched down to Shriver who was writhing in pain.

"I wasn't going to do that for you. I'll be happy to see you behind bars, asshole."

Even though she hurt all over, Ellie couldn't help laughing. She stopped when she became aware of Jordan's worried gaze.

⁓

"He was getting more erratic by the minute, so knew I had to take my chances. And then Jordan appeared like an angry Goddess saving the day…"

"All right, Harding, I get the picture," Carroll interrupted her, though he sounded relieved. He had reason to. "No, I mean that literally. Let's stick to what happened. And while we're at it, do you two know how to take a weekend?"

"Sir? We arrested Shriver, finally," Jordan felt the need to remind him, even though she, too, winced at Ellie's unusually poetic description of the events. "We were lucky Ariel Crane could get to the camp and notify the police. He took the witness's phone and locked her in the store."

"You are all over the place. I'm not used to it, and it worries me. You come back on Monday and write me up the report. No urban fantasy please. And have someone drive you home. I believe Henderson and Doss are still somewhere around here."

"We'll do that, Sir. Thank you."

"Ellie?"

When they had left his office, Jordan asked, "Angry Goddess, really?"

"I did say that, didn't I?" Ellie looked a tad mortified. "With that lightning bolt, the timing was perfect. Your timing was. I'm pretty sure I could have taken him on—"

She didn't state the obvious, that they couldn't say for sure what would have happened. Regardless of their audience, she folded Ellie into a close embrace.

Even though Jordan had insisted she could drive, Derek and Maria had ended up spending a part of the evening.

"People only come to our house for food, drinks and to play with our kid," Ellie observed as they were standing in the kitchen area.

"We heard that," Maria called from where she was sitting on the couch, Meri on her lap. "It might be true. You have a nice place, and this little girl reminds us not everything is going to hell in a handbasket."

Jordan laughed. "It's been one hell of a weekend for sure. You and Val changed your mind?"

"No way," Maria said, handing Meri to Derek. It was a bit past Meri's bedtime, but she looked happy with the company and nowhere near tired. Derek looked pensive. None of their business, Jordan reminded herself.

"Whatever you say. I'm afraid this little girl needs to say good-bye now."

"And just like that, we're back to scary adult stuff," she heard Maria say when she was already in the hallway. "That talk about budget cuts doesn't seem to end."

"Yeah," Derek agreed. "Nothing easier than enjoying the weekend when that's hanging over your head. We still have a lot of payments on that boat."

Once upstairs, Meri didn't seem to mind going through the familiar motions of getting ready for bed, the ritual comforting for her as it was to Jordan who felt safe enough to look at the crazy unexpected turn of this day.

She had needed a win.

However, she didn't want anyone she loved to be in danger of getting there. Today, she had no choice. She'd stepped up and done what needed to be done.

Angry Goddess. She was never going to live that down. But a little flattery hurt no one, and they could finally close the book on Shriver.

"Looks like Mommy's still got it."

Meri giggled, which made her smile. "Thanks for the vote of confidence."

Jordan waited until Meri was asleep, then a few minutes more, before she joined her friends.

About the Author

B arbara Winkes writes sapphic crime drama and Christ-
mas romance. She loves writing characters who get the
job done, whether it's stopping a predator or saving cherished
traditions—while still making time for love. She lives with her
wife in Quebec City.

barbarawinkes.com

Also by Barbara Winkes

Luce Allen Mysteries
In Harm's Way
Under Pressure

The Crossing Lines Trilogy
Undercover
Redemption
Vengeance

The Connected Series
Promised to the Queen
Drawn to the Enemy
Tempted by the Protector
Saved by the Heiress

Carpenter/Harding
Indiscretions
Insinuations
Incisions
Intrusions

BARBARA WINKES

Initiations
Intentions
Infatuations
Impressions
Implications
Infractions
Incidents
Illusions

Kelli & Merin Romantic Suspense
Thunder
Rain

Lord and Burton
Clean Slate

Standalone
The Amnesia Project